Camilla Isley is an e
after she quit her job
in an adventure abroad.

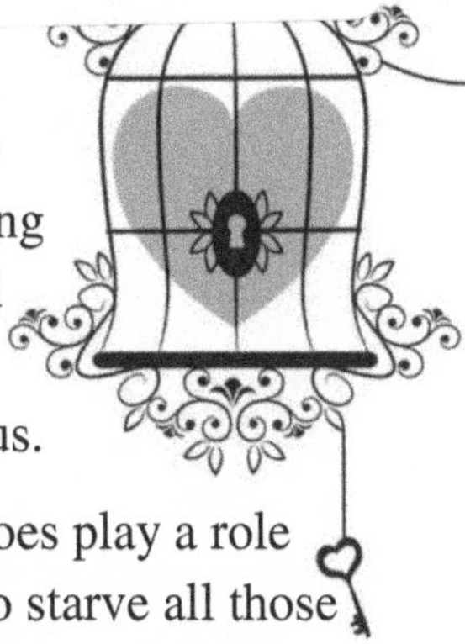

She's a cat lover, coffee addict, and shoe hoarder. Besides writing, she loves reading —duh!—cooking, watching bad TV, and going to the movies—popcorn, please. She's a bit of a foodie, nothing too serious.

A keen traveler, Camilla knows mosquitoes play a role in the ecosystem, and she doesn't want to starve all those frog princes out there, but she could really live without them.

You can find out more about her here: camillaisley.com and by following her on Twitter or Facebook.

@camillaisley
facebook.com/camillaisley

By The Same Author

Romantic Comedies

Standalones

I Wish for You
A Sudden Crush

First Comes Love Series

Love Connection
I Have Never
A Christmas Date
To the Stars and Back
From Thailand with Love

New Adult College Romance

Just Friends Series

Let's Be Just Friends
Friend Zone
My Best Friend's Boyfriend
I Don't Want to be Friends

Love Connection

(A Second Chance Romantic Comedy)

First Comes Love
Book 1

Camilla Isley

This is a work of fiction. Names, characters, businesses, places, events and incidents either are products of the author's imagination or are used fictitiously. Any resemblance to actual events or locales or persons, living or dead, is entirely coincidental.

ISBN-13: 978-8887269048
ISBN-10: 8887269048

Dedication

To my soul mate.

Zero

♥♦♥♦♥♦

Saturday, June 10—New York, JFK Airport

"You've been staring at those two plane tickets for almost an hour now. My role as bartender compels me to ask: what's the big dilemma?"

I stare at the guy behind the bar for the first time since I sat on this stool an hour ago. He has a broad smile and a friendly face.

"If you stop pretending to be drying glasses just to peek at my tickets and pour me another drink," I say, "I'll tell you."

"Sambuca, with ice?"

I nod and shift my attention back to my tickets. Maybe if I stare at them hard enough, the letters will magically move and spell out a solution for me. In the background, I can hear ice tinkle as it hits the bottom of a glass, then crack when the bartender pours the Sambuca. These sounds mingle with the general noises of the airport: flight announcements, passengers chatting, and luggage rolling on the floor.

"Here you go." The bartender sets my drink on the glassy surface of the bar in front of me.

"You added coffee beans," I observe. "Nice touch."

"Pleased to please. But isn't 7 a.m. a little too early for double heavy spirits?"

"I'm on U.K. time, and believe me, I need the double heavy spirits."

"Which brings us back to the tickets. I've earned an explanation."

I sip my Sambuca and take a closer look at the guy's face.

Young—mid-twenties, I'd say. Short sandy hair, intelligent eyes, and always the big smile. He's back at his occupation of drying glasses that don't need drying. Probably one of those people incapable of standing still with nothing to do.

I swirl the ice in my glass. "Is this on the house?"

"On the house, along with the free advice."

"All right," I say. "One ticket's for San Francisco, the other one for Chicago. There're two weddings today, and I need to choose which one to go to."

"Two close friends?"

A loud public announcement blasts through the airport's speaker system, and I wait for it to be over before answering…

One

Two Weddings

I listen to the public announcement while mulling over how to better explain my dilemma.

"All passengers. Flight AA309, with destination Miami has been canceled due to a fire at Miami International Airport. All subsequent flights with destination Miami MIA will also be canceled today. Please go to your airlines' help desk to receive more information on how to reach your final destination. We're sorry for the inconvenience."

On the screen behind the bartender, a report about the chaos at Miami International Airport is taking over the news. The screen reads that the fire has been contained with no casualties, but the airport will sustain heavy delays throughout the day.

"Looks like they're having troubles in Miami," I say, jerking my chin toward the screen.

"Trying to change the subject, are we? You're not going to make me beg for your story, are you?"

"No, you're right."

"So two tickets, two weddings. Are you trying to decide which friend to let down?"

I sigh. "In a way."

"But do both your friends expect you to show up? I mean, don't you usually need to RSVP months in advance for this kind of thing?"

"Mmm, this wedding..." I push the Chicago ticket forward. "I'm supposed to be the maid of honor. This wedding…" I slide the San Francisco ticket next to its twin on the countertop. "I'm not invited."

The bartender snorts. "Seems pretty straightforward to me. Why would you want to bail on a friend to go to a wedding you're not invited to?"

I look him in the eyes. "To stop it from happening."

"Woo-oh. And the plot thickens. My morning just got a lot more interesting than I was expecting. Is it about a guy? Is he the one who got away?"

"Yep." I take another swig of Sambuca; it burns my throat as I swallow. "You don't make burgers here, by any chance? I'm starving."

"Burgers at seven in the morning?"

"I told you, I'm on U.K. time. And burgers are my favorite."

"Sorry, but the kitchen's closed. I can give you some tortilla chips." He opens a new bag and pours them into a wooden bowl. "So, what's his name?"

"Jake."

"Jake." The bartender pauses. "The name has appeal."

"Not just the name." I sigh.

"You want to tell me what happened?"

"We first dated in high school. After graduation, he wanted to go to Stanford, and I wanted to go to Harvard."

The bartender whistles. "The war of the Ivy Leagues. What do you guys do?"

"I'm a lawyer. He's a surgeon."

"So what happened? You fought over schools, went your separate ways, and drifted apart during college?" he asks, his tone saying, *"Same old, same old."*

"No. I went to Stanford instead, to be with him. He assured me we'd go to Harvard for grad school."

"Oh. I sense that promise didn't come true. So you stayed

together through college as well. And…?"

"Stanford offered him a scholarship for Med School. Everything paid for. No student loans, no living expenses. It was an offer no one could've refused."

"And that's when you broke up?"

"No, not yet. I hadn't applied to Stanford Grad School, so for me, it was either lose one year or move to Boston. Harvard was my dream, Stanford his. It wouldn't have been fair for either of us to have to give up our dream school."

"So you left?"

"Yeah. We spent the summer in California and I moved to Boston at the beginning of the fall term. We thought three years apart would be manageable. That's when we found out why everyone says long distance relationships don't work. School was demanding for both of us and catching a six-hour flight over the weekend became more and more difficult. We settled on leading different lives. We were used to sharing everything. Every day, every moment. Suddenly, we both had this huge chunk of life with different things in it. Things the other couldn't understand or get excited about. It was hard. We started arguing, and…"

"And?"

"Depends who you ask. If you asked Jake, he'd probably tell you it was a miscommunication issue. He'd say I overreacted to him telling me about a job offer he'd received in San Francisco. If you asked me, I'd give you a slightly different version…"

"Was your career really that important?" the bartender asks.

"It wasn't that I valued my career over my relationship with Jake. It was the sensation of always coming in second after *his* career. I'd given up my college dream for him. I'd waited all of graduate school… it was his turn to put me first.

To put *us* first."

"If he's still in San Francisco, what's made you change your mind now about being together?"

"I'm not sure I *have* changed my mind."

"So why buy a ticket to San Francisco if you're not even sure you want to try to work things out with him?"

"It was a rash, stupid decision. When I found out Jake was getting married, I panicked. My first thought was that I couldn't let him do it."

"So what's changed?"

"I cooled off and thought about it."

"And?"

"And I realized flying to San Francisco and confronting him was crazy. I mean, what are the odds, really, of us getting back together? I live in London, and he lives in San Francisco. I haven't seen him in forever. I know nothing about his life. We ruined everything once already. How can we possibly make it work this time?"

"And yet here you are, staring at a ticket to San Francisco and contemplating crashing his wedding."

"I can't stop asking myself the 'what if?' question. I'm tired of living in a world of what ifs."

"Meaning?"

"I might've been a tad unreasonable after our break up," I admit.

"As in?"

"As in I moved to the other side of the world and ignored all his calls, emails, and messages. I wanted a fresh start, so I cut him out completely."

The bartender grabs the now-empty wooden bowl and refills it with tortilla chips. "Why?" he asks.

"I was sure he could talk me into moving back to San Francisco if I gave him the chance."

"And you didn't want to quit your job for him?"

"I couldn't. I owed it to myself to make the best choice for *my* career. But the fact remains that moving to the other side of the world didn't help much in forgetting him. I'm still in love with him. He's the only one I ever loved."

"How long ago was this?"

"Three years."

"And you haven't seen him or spoken to him since then?"

"I'm a mess, I know."

"How did you find out he was getting married?"

"Amelia told me—my best friend, the other one getting married today. Amelia, Jake and I are all from a small town near Chicago. She moved to London after getting her bachelor degree and she lives there with her soon-to-be-husband William. But she wanted to get married at home. Anyway, Amelia and Jake had some guests in common, they told Amelia about Jake's wedding as they'd already RSVP'd 'Yes' to him."

"Do you know the girl he's marrying?"

"No." I shake my head decisively. "I don't know anything about her, and I've forced myself not to search Google for intel."

"Aren't you curious?"

"*Yes*. But I can't give her a face. I'd never be able to crash her wedding if I did. She has to stay a ghost."

"When are the weddings?"

"This afternoon."

"Whoa. What's so special about June 10 that everyone wants to get married today? And you're hard-core. Shouldn't you have tried to talk to the guy a little sooner? Are you literally going to barge into the church and yell 'STOP!' in the middle of the ceremony?"

"I'd decided not to go at all."

"But you brought the ticket all the way from London, just in case."

"I did. Having the ticket, even if I knew I wasn't going to use it, made me feel calmer."

"And now you've changed your mind?"

"I don't know. I have no idea what I'm doing."

"When does the plane leave?"

"Which one?"

"Tell me both times."

"San Francisco's eight thirty. Chicago's ten forty-five."

"So you have less than…" He pauses to look at his watch. "Twenty minutes before they start boarding for San Francisco."

"That's correct."

"What's Amelia's take on the situation?"

"She got mad at me at first for even thinking about ditching her wedding. But then again, she's always been a huge fan of Gemma and Jake."

"Gemma?"

"That's me. We all grew up on the same street, and we've been friends forever. Anyway, she's marshaled a back-up maid of honor and she told me to follow my heart."

"And what does your heart say?"

"My heart's telling me it loves Jake. But this is too big. As you said, I can't run into the church and beg him to cancel the wedding."

"What time's the wedding?"

"Six p.m."

"What time does your plane land?"

I look at the ticket. "Noon."

"So you'd have plenty of time to get there before the ceremony starts."

"Mmm, I'm not so sure. The wedding's in some fancy

winery in Napa."

"That's barely an hour's drive. You'll still have all the time you need to get there and talk to him before he goes to the altar."

"But what am I going to say?"

"Say that you love him."

"And?"

"Nothing else. If he's in love with you, it'll be enough."

"Say he doesn't laugh in my face and tell me to leave. Say he admits he still loves me. It doesn't change anything. I'm still in London, and he's still in San Francisco."

"You'll figure something."

"I'm not so sure."

"You said it yourself: you don't want to live in a world of what ifs, right? So it seems pretty obvious you have to try."

"But I'm so scared."

"Do you have anything to lose?"

"No, not really."

"Then why not go?"

"What if he doesn't love me anymore?"

"Then he doesn't, and it will suck, but at least you'll have your answer. But if you don't go, and you don't ask, you'll never know, and you'll regret it for the rest of your life. If you love him, go."

My face becomes suddenly hot and an electric prickle spreads from my heart to my fingertips. "Right. What's the worst that could happen?"

"They could arrest you for crashing a private party. Or the bride could sue you for emotional damages. Or…"

"I'm a lawyer; I can take care of myself in the law department. Are you on my side or what?"

"Of course I am. So, what's the next step?"

"A car. I'm going to need a car in San Francisco. I need

to rent a car." My pulse is racing. I pick up my phone and tap away frantically. "Uhhuuuhhhu. It's done. I did it. I've booked a car. I'm really doing this. Oh gosh. I'm doing it! Is it too lame if I want to high five you?"

"No, not at all." He raises his palm. "Shoot away."

I slam my hand into his. "I have to tell Amelia so she can get her maid-of-honor-plan-B rolling."

"All passengers. Flight UA 730, with destination San Francisco, is beginning boarding at gate B 25. We're going to start boarding families with small kids and passengers with special needs. Then, we're going to board first and business class passengers. And finally, all other passengers…"

"That's your flight they just announced."

"It's my flight. I'm going." I fumble with my bag and carry-on luggage and almost fall from the stool. "How much do I owe you?"

"It's on the house."

"Everything?"

"Yeah. You go tell your man you love him. Go catch your love connection."

"Thank you. Thank you so much." I hurry toward the gate.

"Hey," the bartender calls after me. "Let me know how it goes! I'm on Facebook."

"What's your name?" I shout back without stopping.

"I'm Mark Cooper. And you?"

"Gemma Dawson."

Two

One Choice

♦♦♦

I listen to the public announcement while mulling over how to better explain my dilemma.

"All passengers. Flight AA309, with destination Miami will begin boarding shortly. Please proceed to gate B 36."

On the screen behind the bartender, a report about a near fire at Miami International Airport is taking over the news.

"Looks like they had a close call in Miami," I say, jerking my chin toward the screen.

"Trying to change the subject, are we? You're not going to make me beg for your story, are you?"

"No, you're right."

"So two tickets, two weddings. Are you trying to decide which friend to let down?"

I'm about to lunch into my explanation when a female flight attendant with long strawberry hair interrupts me.

"Please don't talk to me about weddings. Not today." She plonks herself on the stool next to mine and says, "Mark, can I have a drink? Make it strong, please."

She's remarkably beautiful. Tall, with amazing lips and flawless skin. But her blue eyes are filled with so much sadness.

"What's up with you ladies and drinking so early in the morning?" the bartender asks.

"I don't give a damn about the time," the flight attendant says. "I've changed so many time zones in the past week, I'm not even sure if it's day or night for me."

"Did I miss something?" Mark asks in mock shock. "Is I-can-drink-at-7-a.m.-because-I-have-jet-lag the new black?"

"I just need something to calm my nerves and survive the day," the flight attendant pleads. "Make it a shot, please. Quick and painless."

"What happened to you, love?" Mark asks her. "You've got a dark aura today."

They seem to know each other well.

"The whole of Miami Airport almost went into shutdown today. An idiot started a fire, but the firemen caught it before it spread and everything was solved quickly. Otherwise, I would've been stuck in that swamp for the entire weekend."

"Oh, come on, darling. Miami's hardly a swamp. What's really up with you?"

"Nothing. Is my drink ready?"

"Give me a sec." Mark starts fumbling with various bottles and a shaker. Who knew you could put so much work into a shot? "Aren't you supposed to go home, honey?"

"Too depressing. I might drink myself to death if I go home now. At least here you can keep tabs on me."

"Will do, but for now… here's your drink. A pink starburst shot for the nerves."

I'm kind of jealous. My Sambuca, albeit with coffee beans, looks a little beginner problems-of-the-heart-at-7-a.m.-drinker next to the pink starburst. At least, I'm assuming the flight attendant is going through a heartbreak. Nothing else could drive a seemingly non-AA woman to drinking so early in the morning. I should know.

Anyway, I don't have much time to admire the pretty pink starburst. As soon as Mark puts the glass on the bar, she grabs it and drains it in a single swig.

"Better?" he asks.

"A little bit."

The vodka did add some color to her previously ghastly cheeks.

"Is this dark mood about your professor?" Mark prompts.

The word professor has barely left his lips before the flight attendant starts sobbing her heart out. She's hiccupping one word for every two or three sighs.

"Never… if… mine… engaged all along… wedding… today… she blonde…"

Mark looks at her, eyes wide, mouth slightly open. "You may have to repeat that, sweetheart."

I should be offended that my own wedding troubles have taken a back seat in the conversation, but this girl seems to be doing a lot worse. Plus, I could use a break from my ticket staring.

"Tissue," she pleads.

Mark offers her a paper napkin, and she blows her nose loudly. After a few more sobs, she seems calm enough to speak.

"William," she says, spitting the name in a way that tells me she hates and loves the guy at the same time. "He's been engaged all this time. Never had the guts to tell me until he was practically at the altar. Too bad men don't wear engagement rings. We should shackle a band on their fingers—an irremovable one—the moment they propose. At least that way they couldn't walk the world free to string along perfectly innocent, stupidly over-trusting naïve girls like me."

Ouch. She's really having it rough.

"Engaged?" Mark asks. "But how's that possible? You've been with him… how long?"

"A year!" the flight attendant wails. "Twelve months

down the drain. Bam, just like that. A year of my life, wasted. I was already seeing him as the father of my unborn babies, and he's probably going to make one with another woman. Tonight!" If she were a cat, she'd be wheezing. "He always said he couldn't stay in New York for the weekends. Remember how he always flew back to London the minute his last class of the week ended? It was because he had a fiancée to go back to. And she's blonde."

"Do we hate her?"

"No, we don't hate her. She doesn't have any fault in this. She's getting married to a lying, cheating, sorry excuse for a man, and she doesn't have a clue."

"Don't you think she *should* have a clue? It sounds to me as if she's marrying a man she doesn't know. How could she not suspect anything?"

"Same applies to me. I didn't suspect anything. I didn't have the slightest clue. Believe me, he's that good."

"Esther, I'm so sorry," Mark says. "I thought the professor was The One."

"Me too."

"How did you find out?"

"The bastard told me. Two weeks ago. He just said it: 'I'm sorry, I'm getting married in two weeks. I thought I'd have the strength to call it off, but I don't. I love you, but I can't see you anymore.' That's what he had the guts to tell me. More or less. In one awkward conversation, I was gone from his life."

"But you really never had a teeny tiny suspicion? Didn't you check his Facebook profile?"

"He doesn't use Facebook. He says it wouldn't be dignified for a professor."

"Ah, never trust a guy who doesn't have a Facebook

profile."

What a bastard. How can anyone do something like that? Why get married if you're already cheating? It doesn't make sense. It's like adding Mexican chili peppers to a dish when you can't digest spicy food.

"And he said he loved you."

Esther nods.

"Do you think he was lying?"

"The worst part is that I'm almost sure he wasn't."

"But, darling, this whole story doesn't make sense. If he says he loves you, why would he go get married to another woman?"

"He said he's been with her for a long time. He said he tried to call it off, but every time he was about to tell her, he panicked. In the end, he said he just couldn't do it. So today, he's marrying her in Chicago. She's from a small town nearby. I Googled her. She *does* have Facebook. Her name's Amelia. She's blonde and beautiful. And today she's going to become Mrs. William Reilly."

Amelia and William Reilly. As she says the names, a bolt of electricity runs through me. Amelia, my blonde best friend, is getting married today in Chicago to William Reilly. He's a professor at London Business School. He also has a job at Columbia University where he teaches Financial Markets one week every month. And he doesn't use Facebook because he thinks it wouldn't be dignified for a scholar. It's one coincidence too many.

I try to stay calm and not show the shock on my face when I oh-so-casually butt in.

"What did you say this guy, the professor, taught?" I ask.

The bartender and the girl turn toward me as if they've both just remembered I'm here.

"Excuse me. Who are you?" the flight attendant asks, unable to keep the hostility from her voice.

"Gemma Dawson, nice to meet you," I say with a warm smile. "I apologize for interrupting, but I couldn't help overhearing your conversation."

"Esther Porter." She offers a manicured hand, which I shake. "And *I* should apologize. I'm being rude for no reason."

"Mark Cooper," the bartender chips in.

We do an awkward round of nice-to-meet-yous.

"Why did you want to know what he teaches?" Esther asks. "What difference does it make?"

Since I can't exactly tell her the truth, I blab the first excuse that comes to my mind. "I read this study once, which said people who work with numbers—finance people in particular—have a tendency to live duplicitous lives." I can't believe the load of crap that's exiting my mouth. But I need to know for sure if she's talking about Amelia's William.

"That's absolutely true!" Mark exclaims. "Didn't your professor teach Financial Markets at Columbia?"

"Yeah," Esther confirms. "I'm glad to know there's a clinical explanation for his being a cheating, double-crossing bastard."

My heart sinks. How many William Reillys commuting from London to New York to teach Financial Markets at Columbia could there be? Just one, I'm afraid.

"All passengers. Flight UA 730, with destination San Francisco, is beginning boarding at gate B 25. We're going to start boarding families with small kids and passengers with special needs. Then, we're going to board first and business class passengers. And finally, all other passengers…"

I hear the announcement for the San Francisco flight and my heart plummets. I can't go. I can't abandon Amelia and let her marry that scum. If I needed a clearer sign Jake and I aren't meant to be together, this is it. I'm not going to San Francisco; I'm not stopping his wedding. I feel my heart break in my chest and I lean on the bar countertop for support.

"Are you okay?" Mark asks me. "You look as if you've seen a ghost!"

"Yeah, yeah. I'm fine. I just need to use the restroom. How much do I owe you?"

"Don't worry, it's on the house."

"Everything?" I ask, surprised.

"Yeah, don't worry," he says with a big smile. "Hey, we never finished our chat about those plane tickets."

"It doesn't matter anymore," I tell him, tearing the ticket for San Francisco in two and throwing it in the bin at the end of the bar. "The universe just decided for me. Thanks again." I wave goodbye to Mark and turn toward Esther. "I know it's not much, but I hope you'll find someone who deserves you."

"Thank you," she sighs. "Have a safe trip."

I wave goodbye again, grab my hand luggage and shuffle away from the bar toward the screens with the Departures information.

"This is the last call for Flight UA 730, with destination San Francisco. All passengers, please go to gate B 25 for boarding. The gate will be closing in five minutes. I repeat, this is the last call for flight UA 730 with destination San Francisco."

Hearing the announcement is like having a jackhammer pointing to my chest and digging into my heart. It's shattering everything it finds in its way, leaving nothing behind. Just a giant empty hole. I'm letting Jake go, I realize with a flip of my stomach. I wipe a single tear from my cheek and stare at the screen, shaking the heartbreak away. I don't have time to mourn the loss of the love of my life right now; I have a job to do. There will be plenty of time to cry later—like, the rest of my life.

Right. I stare at the panel. The flight for Chicago departs from Gate A 47. I head there. While I walk, I take out my phone and search on Google for the phone number of Columbia University. Before I crash into Amelia's wedding screaming, "He's a cheater!" I need to have my facts straight.

After some pushing around of privacy laws, I finally manage to speak directly with the Business Department Dean. He confirms that only one William Reilly teaches Financial Markets at Columbia and commutes from London once a month.

I sit on a plush chair at the gate and text Amelia to tell her I'll make it to her wedding. I tell her to wait for me at all costs before she starts the ceremony. She texts back a shower of smiling emoticons and I can't help but feel miserable for being about to ruin her life. Only, I'm not the one ruining her life. The bastard is. Right. I'm saving her from living unhappily ever after. This is the attitude I need to keep for the rest of the day. There's no way stopping her wedding isn't the right thing to do. She will understand. She has to. I just hope she's not going to hate me for it. I was never a believer in, "Don't shoot the messenger."

Three

Speak Now

♥♥♥

Saturday, June 10—New York, JFK Airport

"Good Morning, ladies and gentlemen, this is your captain speaking. I'm glad to inform you we're about to take off. The weather's clear today and we should be able to land in San Francisco right on time. I wish you a pleasant flight."

I relax back in my seat, relieved to hear we're on schedule. I don't have much of a buffer as it is—if I want to get to the winery before the ceremony starts, everything needs to go smoothly. I just wish I weren't trapped on a plane for six hours with only my crazy thoughts to keep me company. My body might start a rebellion. I haven't slept in a day, and the idea of crashing Jake's wedding is pumping so much adrenaline in me, I'm ready to explode. I feel worse than a beer can in an automatic shaker. I grab the armrest as the plane gathers speed on the runway and takes off.

As soon as the seatbelt sign switches off, I fish in my bag for a notepad and a pen. I like to organize my thoughts in writing. When I have a speech to give, I always prefer to follow a script. Speaking off the cuff makes me nervous, so I start jotting down some marry-me-instead speech ideas.

Dear Jake,

Mmm, I'm not really writing a letter, though.

Jake,

Yeah, that's better. A strong, assertive start.

Jake,
I've known you my entire life and I've been in love with you for most of my adult life.

Adult life? Who says adult life? It's not romantic enough. I need to remind myself I'm not writing a harangue but an undying love declaration.

Jake,
I'm just a girl standing in front of a boy...

Overkill? Maybe I should keep it simpler and less cheesy.

Jake,
Ditch the biatch and marry me instead!

Short, concise, says all one needs to know. Pity I can't really use it.

***

By the time we land in San Francisco, I've reached speech draft number eighteen and I've still no clue what I'm going to say to Jake. On the other hand, my brain's positively fried. As I don't have to claim any luggage—I'm traveling light—I head straight to the car rental to pick up my car.

At the concierge, there's a bit of a line—five people before me in total. Damn. I hate waiting in line. Especially after the traveling and lack of sleep. I hope all the good cars won't be gone by the time my turn arrives. The clerk seems a super slow and fastidious one. It takes her forty-five minutes to sort through the customers before she finally gets to me.

"Good morning. I need your name, driving license, and credit card, please."

"I'm Gemma Dawson; I've made an online reservation."

"Yes, I have your booking in the server for a three-day

rental. Is that correct?"

"Correct."

"Just a second." She types away at her keyboard. "Would you like to add insurance, ma'am?"

"Yes, please."

"All right, your credit card has already been charged for the rental amount when you booked online. I'll add insurance and charge a deposit fee of five hundred dollars. The deposit won't be withdrawn from your account, but it'll be on hold, meaning it won't be available for you to spend. Once you return the car, the amount will be made available to you in two business days to a week. Is that okay with you?"

"Yeah, sure." Deposit, plus insurance, plus the rental itself, plus the plane tickets. These will max out my credit card. I should have brought more cash.

"Okay, the credit card's taken care of. You can have it back." She slides it across the counter. "I just need to input the last few details for the insurance..."

"Sure."

"Oh."

Oh? What is she oh-ing about? I want 'very well' or 'here are your keys', not 'oh.'

"Is there a problem?" I ask, on edge. This is taking way too long.

"I'm afraid so, madam. I apologize; I should've checked before. Your driver's license appears to have expired."

"What do you mean, 'expired'? That's impossible!"

"Madam, it says here it expired a month ago."

I check the expiration date. "Oh, gosh!" My palms get clammy at once.

"Have you been driving with this?"

"No, no. I live in London. Nobody drives there."

"A U.K. driving license would be fine too."

"I don't have a U.K. driving license; I'd never be able to drive on the wrong side of the road with no casualties."

"If you don't have a valid license, I can't rent you a car."

"But I need to go to Napa! How will I get there without a car?"

Why is this happening to me? Today of all days.

"I'm sure you'll find a cab outside. It shouldn't cost you more than the rental. I'll need your credit card back to issue a refund."

"Here." I take the card out of my wallet and pass it to her.

A minute later, she hands it back. "The refund has been issued and the funds will be available to you in two business days to a week."

"Two business days?" I exclaim, bewildered. "You mean to say that my card's still maxed out?"

"If today's charge maxed it out, yes. It will stay that way until Tuesday at the very least."

"Can't you issue a refund in cash?"

"No, madam, we're not an A.T.M."

"So now I don't have a car, and you've taken the money to pay for the cab. What am I supposed to do?"

"There's a train to the city, and I'm sure you'll be able to find a bus to Napa, but we're not a tourist office. Now, I kindly need you to step aside so I can serve our next customer. Have a nice day."

"You too," I say. *Rot in hell*, I think.

***

Two trains, three buses, and four hours later I finally arrive in Yountville, the town in Napa where my final bus stops. With all the connections, I barely managed to close my eyes for half an hour here and there. I'm exhausted. But I'm not giving up. I'm a woman on a mission.

I look around the deserted bus stop to see if I can find a taxi station. Jake's getting married in some sort of fancy castle in the area, and I need someone to take me there. Yountville looks like a cross between an Old West outpost, a French country town, and a Disney park—thanks to a garden of stone mushrooms on the side of the main road. Maybe tapping one would turn them into the cutesy trolls from *Frozen*.

Mushroom trolls aside, the town looks desolate. No cars zooming on the street, no passersby, no one. The only open place seems to be a red brick building with an ivy-covered wall that looks like a shopping mall. I head there to ask for some information and enter a chocolate shop with the cutest truffles you'll ever see on display. A nice looking girl is standing behind the counter leafing through a magazine. She looks up as a bell above the door chimes, announcing my arrival.

"Hello. How may I help you today? Are you looking for a present?"

"Err, no. Actually, I was wondering where I could find a cab."

"Oh."

Another oh. I don't like ohs.

"You won't be lucky today," she says. "It's wedding season, and all the taxis are working as shuttle services, booked way in advance. You'll hardly find one passing by."

"But how do people get to weddings if they don't have a car?"

"Ah, well. Usually, transportation's arranged by the bride and groom. Are you going to a wedding?"

"Yes, at the Castello di Amorosa."

"What hotel are you staying in?"

"I'm not exactly staying in a hotel. I just arrived."

She gives me a puzzled look.

"I wasn't supposed to come," I explain. "I changed my mind at the last minute, but I need to get there quickly. The wedding starts in one hour."

"You're going dressed like that?" she asks even more suspiciously, narrowing her eyes at me.

I stare down at my crumpled blouse, jeans, and traveling flats. "*Yes*. I'm going dressed like this because, guess what, I'm not a guest. Okay? I'm not even invited if you really must know." All the stress, the fatigue of the past twenty-four hours, is finally bubbling out. The shaken beer can has been opened. "But I need to get to that wedding before it starts. And I need to get there fast as it's my intention to steal the groom *before* he gets married. So if you could please tell me if there are any means of transportation I could use to get there, I'd be eternally in your debt."

The girl claps her hands and squeals, "You should've told me that in the first place. Nothing this exciting has ever happened to me." I refrain from pointing out that nothing's really happening to *her* and let her babble on. "You're going to be the talk of the town. Stealing the groom, like in the movies. This is so romantic!"

"So, can you help me?"

"Of course. I'm Jody, nice to meet you."

"Gemma." I shake her hand.

"Let me call my brother. He has to go there to deliver some hay; there's a pretty farm near the castle. I'll see if he can give you a ride."

***

"Are you all right back there?" Jody's brother, Mike, shouts from the cab of his tractor half an hour later.

"Yeah, I'm fine," I shout back. At least as fine as I'll ever be riding on the back of a noisy tractor, perched on a stack of hay bales. It turns out Jody's brother drives a one-seater tractor.

If this was a chick flick, I'd be thoroughly enjoying watching the adventures of the female lead as she struggles to reach her one true love. But I've never been more aware of how much TV can make anything appear cool, when *it's not*. Like riding on the back of a tractor. And this not being a movie, I'm not even sure it won't all have been for nothing.

As the castle gets closer, I worry less about if I'm going to get there in time, and more about what Jake's reaction will be. Does he still love me? What will he say? Will we look into each other's eyes and run away into the sunset, holding hands? I hope he'll look me *only* in the eyes, as the rest of my body can't be much to look at right now. I probably smell too, and the hayride isn't helping.

The tractor stops. "All right," Mike shouts, killing the engine. "We're here. I can't go up the hill with this, but there's the parking lot, and the entrance is just behind it."

I hop off.

"You need help with the bag?" Mike asks.

"No, I'm fine, thank you," I say, pulling my trolley bag off the hay. "Thanks again! You saved my life."

"Good luck," Mike yells, before restarting the tractor and blowing a dark cloud of exhaust on me. Just about all the freshening up I need.

I check the time on my phone; it's already past six. The ceremony must be underway. There goes my plan of a discreet talk before everything started. I guess it'll be "burst inside and yell in the middle of the ceremony" instead. I hurry up the hill, dragging my hand language behind me, and reach the castle's entrance.

There's a guy guarding the door.

"I'm sorry, madam, we're closed for a private event today."

"Yes, I'm here for the wedding," I say nonchalantly.

The guy eyes me suspiciously. "You have an invitation?"

"Sure," I lie, and open my trolley to pretend to look for it inside. "I can't seem to find it right now… I'm already late. Is there any chance you could let me pass? The ceremony must've started by now."

"I'm sorry, madam, I need to see an invitation before I can let you through."

"Sure, I'll find it. I'm sure it's here somewhere." I try to appear calm and unconcerned, but inside I'm panicking. What if this guy doesn't let me in? Will I be on the other side of the wall while Jake says, "I do"? How pathetic would that be? No, it can't happen. I came here from the other side of the world; I won't have this stupid, sorry excuse for a bouncer keep me out. I need a distraction; just a few seconds to have him drop his guard so I can slip through the door.

I'm still rummaging inside my luggage when an idea hits me. I position the trolley bag so that the wheels are facing downhill and push it. The bag rolls down the slope, sprawling some of my clothes along the way. I yell in surprise and bouncer guy instinctively runs after the rolling bag. As soon as he turns his back, I duck inside the castle.

I run down a random corridor, having no idea where I'm going or where the ceremony's being held. Someone shouts behind me, but I don't turn around. I keep running through a pair of wooden doors, under an arcade, and through another door, until I find myself in a square courtyard crowded with many elegantly-laid round tables. They must be for the wedding reception. I'm getting closer, but where is the ceremony?

"You stop right there, miss," bouncer guy yells from

under the arcade. He's running toward me at a menacingly fast pace.

A bunch of closed doors overlooks the courtyard. I slalom through the tables and launch myself at the door straight ahead of me, bursting inside just as bouncer guy catches up with me. I've made it into a frescoed room full of people.

Someone's speaking.

"Should anyone here present know of any reason why this couple should not be joined in matrimony, speak now or forever hold your peace…"

I made it. I'm in.

"Gotcha." Bouncer guy grabs my elbow forcefully.

"STOP!" I yell. "You have to stop! Let me go. Let me *go.*"

Bouncer guy has grabbed me from behind, lifting me from the floor, and he's carrying me outside while I'm kicking my legs furiously in the air. "Stop!" I scream again. "You have to stop. I speak! I want to speak now! STOP!"

"Gemma?"

The groom turns toward me and the entire room falls silent. I freeze, one leg kicked out in midair. If ever someone could master the make-you-feel-like-the-only-person-in-the-room stare, Jake was your man. Suddenly, I don't seem able to talk anymore.

Four

Not Holding Peace

♦♦♦

Saturday, June 10—Chicago Area

"Should anyone here present know of any reason why this couple should not be joined in matrimony, speak now or forever hold your peace…"

"STOP!" I yell at the top of my lungs as I run up the aisle. "I need to speak. Stop. You have to stop." I'm drenched in sweat and panting.

"Gemma?" The groom turns toward me, and the entire room falls silent. I freeze in the middle of the aisle and suddenly I don't seem able to talk anymore. *Because I want to kill the bastard!* I don't trust myself with getting any closer to him.

"Gemma?" Amelia blinks, perplexed. She's resplendent in her white gown. My heart breaks for her. "You made it! What happened to you? I got your text saying you were coming, but you disappeared. You should've landed hours ago. What happened?"

"Long story." I try to catch my breath. "Expired driving license, maxed credit card, public transportation, traffic, chicken trucks…"

The journey here was a nightmare. The resort where Amelia's getting married is lost in the country in the middle of nowhere. I'd tried to rent a car to come here, but it turned out my license had expired and my credit card maxed out. I didn't have enough cash on me for a cab all the way from Chicago, and once I got to the closest town by bus, *there were no cabs*. So the only passage I found was in a truck transporting chickens. I'm sure I still have feathers on me.

"Are you okay?" Amelia asks.

"Mostly…"

"Err-hem." The minister clears his throat in the background. "If you don't mind, miss, we're in the middle of a ceremony here."

"Right." Amelia seems to realize for the first time that I've just interrupted her wedding. "Why don't you take a seat and we can talk later?"

"Actually," I mumble, twisting my fingers, "I need to talk to you right now."

"Can't it wait until later? I'm kind of in the middle of something here," Amelia says, annoyed now.

"Don't you think I know? I need to talk to you *before* you go through with the something. It's important."

"Okay then, say what you've come to say so we can get a move on."

"It'd be better if you could step aside for a second and talk to me in private."

"Gemma, I love you. But I'm getting married, right now. I'm not stepping aside for a girl talk."

Mr. Taylor, Amelia's father, grabs my elbow and drags me gently to the side. "Come on, dear, this can wait until later."

"Let me go," I protest. "Let me go! Amelia, I need to talk to you, seriously, please. Give me five minutes."

"Gemma, I know you have a taste for drama, but today is not the day. We will talk *after* I get married."

"Nooooo!" I scream as Mr. Taylor revives his efforts to drag me away. "You can't marry him, you just can't."

"Have you gone mad?" Amelia screeches. "Why have you decided to ruin this day for me? First, you say you're going to be my maid of honor, then you dump me to run after your ex-boyfriend, then you change your mind again, get here half an hour late, and try to stop the wedding. Why? *Why*?"

"I really think we should talk about it in private."

"If you have something to say, just say it, for goodness' sake."

Amelia's dad chimes in. "Young lady, I've known you your entire life and I've never been more disappointed in you."

"Mr. Taylor, I'm sorry, but I assure you I have a very good reason. Amelia, please. I have something serious I need to tell you, but it's better for you if I don't say it in front of everyone. Trust me on this."

"I've had enough," she snaps. "Dad, can you please take her outside? I'll talk to her later." She turns to talk to the minister. "You can go on."

"Hem, technically…"

"What?" Amelia spits.

"The ritual imposes that when a claim is made, I am to listen to it."

"It's nothing serious, I can assure you," Amelia says caustically, shooting me a furious look. "My friend's jetlagged. We can move forward." Amelia turns to her brother. "Malcolm, get her out of here."

Amelia's brother joins their dad and grabs me from behind, lifting me off the floor. I try to resist, but I can only kick my legs uselessly in the air while he drags me outside.

"Stop, let me go. Even the minister says I should talk. Amelia, please listen to me. You can't marry him. You can't. Let me go!"

As we near the exit door, I panic. They're going to drag me out in five seconds, and Amelia's going to marry that bastard. I can't let it happen. So I blurt my secret out in the worst possible way.

"He's a cheating, lying bastard!" I scream.

There's a general intake of breath from the guests, and Amelia's brother drops me to the ground. I shake him off with some indignation and walk back up the aisle.

"Why are you doing this to me?" Amelia asks, close to tears.

"Because it's true." I'm about to cry myself. "Her name's Esther, she lives in New York, and she works as a flight attendant. He's been having an affair with her for a year, and he called it off two weeks ago because he didn't have the guts to leave you even though he's in love with her. He's been living two lives since he got that teaching job at Columbia. One with you in London and one with her in New York."

"I don't believe you," Amelia hisses.

"If you don't believe me, ask him," I say quietly.

All heads turn toward William. He looks like a corpse. Ghastly skin, bluish bags under his eyes, and hollow cheeks. He doesn't look like someone who's getting married but more like someone who's walking down death row.

"Tell me it's not true," Amelia squeals. "Tell me."

William stares at her, petrified.

"William?"

He finally breaks.

"I'm sorry…"

"Sorry? You're *sorry*?"

"I didn't know how to tell you."

"Tell me? Tell me what, exactly? That you don't love me? That you're in love with someone else? That you cheated on me for a year?"

"I-I'm sorry…"

"No. *NO*. You don't get to be sorry, you bastard."

That's when she goes Carrie-Bradshaw-after-Mr.-Big-leaves-her-at-the-altar crazy and hits William on the head with her bouquet. "You humiliated me," blow. "You cheating," blow. "Lying," blow. "Loser," blow. "I hate you," blow.

Petals fly everywhere. When there's nothing left of the bouquet, Amelia throws it away and stares at the room, disoriented. She catches my gaze and something switches on her face. She runs toward me and I'm afraid I'm going to be next on her hit list, but instead she grabs my hand and pleads, "Get me out of here. Get me out of here as quick as you can."

Hand-in-hand, we run out the door, down the long, carpeted hallway, and burst onto the grassy lawn.

"I don't have a car," I say.

"How did you get here?"

"On a truck full of chickens. Trust me, you don't want to know."

A whistle resounds behind us, and we turn to see Amelia's brother running after us.

"Dad says to take his car." He throws the keys at me and gathers Amelia in a bone-crushing hug. "Call us when you're a little calmer—promise?"

"I promise," Amelia says. "But now I just want to get the hell out of here."

I follow her panicked gaze to the chapel's entrance door where the first guests are streaming outside. I catch a glimpse of my trolley lying against the wall.

"My bag," I say to Malcolm. "I need my bag."

"I'll get it. You get the car around." He hugs me and whispers in my ear, "Thank you, and sorry. We owe you."

I wave him away, embarrassed and close to tears again, and follow Amelia to the car. Malcolm puts my bag in the trunk and bangs his hand on it twice to signal we can go. I push my foot on the accelerator, sending grit flying under the tires as I steal the bride away.

I look at her. She's staring out of the window and I can't see her face.

"I'm sorry I had to tell you this way."

"I can't talk about it. Not yet." Her voice is broken, as is my heart for her.

"Where do you want me to take you?"

"Away. As far away as possible."

"Okay."

I'm not sure what she means, but I'm okay with driving the car until we have a better idea of where we're going. That is until I remember my driving license has expired. I hit the brakes. We're on a road in the middle of a crop field. There's no police here, but once we get to the main road, I can't risk being arrested.

"I'm sorry, but you'll have to drive. My driving license's expired."

"Of course you'd come to steal the bride with an expired license."

Amelia shakes her head, amused. She steps out of the car and becomes immediately serious again as she looks down at herself in her wedding gown, which becomes the next victim of her blind rage. She tears, trashes, and screams. This time, instead of petals, there's crinoline and tulle flying everywhere. When she's accomplished the look of a zombie bride from *Dawn of the Dead*, she starts pulling at the dress like a mad woman.

"Help me. Get it off me. I need it off me."

I run toward her and start undoing all the tiny hooks and buttons on the back.

"It's taking too long. I can't breathe."

"This dress has a thousand buttons."

"I don't care about the buttons—tear it off. Get me out of it."

I rip the fabric apart with some satisfaction and help her slip out of the zombie dress.

She takes a couple of calming breaths before saying, "Clothes. I need clothes." She's wearing only her bridal lingerie. Thank goodness we're in the middle of nowhere. "My honeymoon bag should be in the trunk with yours. I slept at my parents' yesterday."

I open the trunk and fish in her bag for a pair of jeans and a black tank top. She throws off her shoes to get into the jeans, pulls them on, and bends forward to pick up the shoes, which she curve-balls into the field. Okay, I'm going to let it slide and not give her a lecture about littering. Instead, I go back to the trunk and pass her a pair of flats.

She gets out of the field and into the car, I mount shotgun, and we speed away. The sole memento of our passage in this deserted land will be the cadaver of a white satin dress resting in peace at the side of the road.

As we reach more trafficked streets, Amelia makes one sure turn after another. She seems to have a clear idea of where we're going.

"Ames?" I say uncertainly. "Where are we going?"

"How many days do you have off?"

"A week, stretchable."

"Good."

"Why? Where are we going?"

"The airport."

Five

Wedding Inquisition

Saturday, June 10—Napa Valley

"Gemma?" Jake repeats. "Is it you?"

Finally, bouncer guy drops me to the ground. I shake him off with some indignation and walk back toward the center of the room.

"Jake," is all I'm able to say.

On the other hand, the bride doesn't seem to suffer from muteness.

"Jake, who is this woman? Security, can you take her away, please?"

Jake appears shell-shocked.

"Is this Gemma, as in your ex-girlfriend?" the bride asks. "What's she doing here?"

"I don't know," Jake says.

"Tell her to go away. I don't want her here."

I find my voice again. "Jake, I need to talk to you."

Jake stares from me to his wife-to-be and back, still at a loss for words.

"Well, we don't want to hear what you have to say. So you can go," the bride says.

I look pointedly at the minister. "I have a right to speak; everyone can speak. I want to speak now."

"Well, technically, she does have a right to speak," the minister says.

"Oh, please!" The bride's voice jumps up a few octaves as she turns toward the minister to argue. "You're the one who told me the 'speak now or forever hold your peace' was an archaic form with no real value, and that it wasn't necessary anymore."

"But you insisted on keeping it, so now she has a right to speak. It's the protocol."

The bride turns around and gives me the stare of death. I ignore her and turn toward Jake.

"Jake." I inhale deeply. "When I discovered you were getting married, my world collapsed. I bought a ticket for San Francisco the same night, telling myself I was never going to use it, that coming here was a stupid idea, that I'd say the wrong thing and humiliate myself. Then today came, I was at the airport with the ticket in my hands, and I couldn't stay away.

"I couldn't live with myself another day if I didn't do this. I wish I had perfect and beautiful words to say to you, but the truth is I don't. I wrote eighteen speech drafts coming here and now none of them seems to make any sense. All I can think about are the things I should've said three years ago, and I didn't say because I was too stubborn, too proud to admit my mistakes. Too proud to pick up the phone when you were calling. Too proud to reply to your emails. Too proud to admit I was wrong and you were right.

"Well, I'm not anymore. I made so many mistakes, and coming here today is probably going to be the biggest one yet. But the one thing I'm sure wasn't a mistake in my life was—*is* loving you. Because that's what I came to say, I love you… and I'm sorry. I'm sorry for leaving you, I'm sorry for all the wrong choices I made, and I'm sorry for choosing the worst possible day to tell you all this. But I'm not sorry I love you. Knowing I was about to lose you forever made me realize that in the past three years, I've lived my life without being really alive. Because you're what makes me feel alive. You always have been. And I don't care if my life's here, in London, or wherever else, because now I understand that *you* are my life, Jake. Not a job, not a place.

"I've tried not to love you—believe me, I've tried. But I just can't. I don't care if this is lame or embarrassing. I don't care about anything other than you… I thought you should know… what I'm trying to say is just that I love you, I'm in love with you, and I want to be with you."

I finish my speech, and the entire room stays wrapped in an eerie silence. Everything seems frozen in time. The guests look like petrified statues, and Jake's face is inscrutable. I keep looking into his gray eyes, trying to decipher what's going on inside his head. I get lost in his gaze of misty winds, ice, and snowstorms.

That's until the bride breaks the spell. "Well, you've said your piece. Now you can go. Jake, tell her to go."

Jake tears his eyes away from me and stares at the bride.

"Jake," she repeats, her voice shaky, "tell her to *go*."

Jake has his back turned; I can't see his face as he's dropped his head to stare at the floor. When he looks back up at the bride, her face scrunches up in a grimace.

"I can't," Jake says heavily. "I'm sorry."

"You bastard," the bride yells, raising her bouquet above her head. I think she's about to go Carrie-Bradshaw-after-Mr.-Big-leaves-her-at-the-altar crazy and hit Jake on the head with the bouquet, but she must have a change of heart midway because she hurls the bouquet at me instead, screaming, "You bitch!", and runs out of the room.

Instinctively, I duck. The bouquet soars above my head, hitting Jake's mom straight in the face. Why did I duck? I should've taken one for the team. This isn't going to gain me any I'm-a-better-daughter-in-law points. *Stupid reflexes*!

I see Jake murmur something to his younger brother, Edward, who walks toward my side of the room.

"Are you okay, Mom?" he asks Mrs. Wilder.

"Yes, yes."

He kisses her on the cheek, exchanges muffled words with bouncer guy, and turns toward me. "You. With me," he says curtly.

I contemplate protesting, but I need someone in the family on my side. I throw one last glance at Jake, who's whispering furiously with the minister and doesn't turn around. So I follow his brother out of the room.

"Where are we going?" I ask Edward as he turns into a narrow corridor and down a flight of steep stone steps.

"Somewhere more private."

Oh my goodness. He's taking me to the castle dungeons. What next? Is the wedding inquisition coming to interrogate me? Are they going to send bouncer guy?

Edward leads me through a labyrinth of corridors and finally lets me into a small room with walls made of thick stone, no windows, and two doors. The room's furnished with two chairs and an old-fashioned table.

"Wait here," Edward says.

"For whom? How long?"

"Jake, and I'm not sure."

"Please don't leave me here alone."

"You're going to be fine; I have things to sort upstairs." He walks through the door, then pauses and pops his head back into the room. "Ah, Gemma?"

"Yeah?"

"That was bad ass." He winks at me and walks away, closing the door behind him.

I pace around the small cell, but there's not really much I can do besides sitting in one of the chairs. I check my phone—no signal here. Not that I need to call anyone. What's going on upstairs? What's happening? Is the wedding off? It looked that way, but who knows?

Suddenly the door bursts open and Jake storms into the room. With a few flicks of his fingers, he removes his bow tie and sets his gray eyes on me. They're ignited with… umm… emotions. Love? Hate? Anger? Passion? I'm not sure. I can't read his features.

Even with the tortured face, he's impossibly handsome. My eyes flicker over the bow tie hanging loosely around his neck and the open shirt exposing his Adam's apple—too sexy. I move my gaze up to his shaven, strong jaw and back to his icy gray eyes, intimate and foreign at the same time. Three years have chiseled his face, making it even more gorgeous. *Not fair.* No one should look this good.

I make to get up on wobbly knees and go toward him, but he stops me with a raised finger. "Down," he orders, moving the same finger downwards to indicate what I should do.

He starts pacing around the room. He stops, looks at me, and speaks.

"You…" He shakes his head and starts pacing again.

After a few seconds, it's a repeat.

Stops. Looks. Speaks.

"Of all days… *today*!" Shakes head. Starts pacing.

It's like a dance.

Stops. Looks. Speaks.

"Years, Gemma… *years*!" Shakes head. Starts pacing.

Stops. Looks. Speaks.

"Not a word…" Shakes head. Starts pacing.

Stops. Looks. Speaks.

"You're crazy."

He's finally standing still. Umm. I'm tempted to ask if he thinks I'm crazy in a you're-so-cute-because-you're-crazy-romantic way or if it's more of an I-want-them-to-shut-you-in-an-asylum-and-throw-away-the-keys crazy. I make to stand up and join him, but he shows me his index again.

"Down."

"Can't we talk if I stand?"

"No Gemma, we can't. Right now, I need you there at a safe distance. I'm still too mad at you to have you in my air."

"Okay, I'm going to sit down." I feel like Chris Pratt talking to Blue in *Jurassic World.* I'm not sure if Jake is going to tear me to pieces or join #TeamGemma. "But please say something."

"Three years, Gemma. *Three. Years*." He finally seems able to streamline his thoughts in a more articulate way. "Not a word from you in three years, and you choose my wedding day to have a chat?"

"I'm sorry, Jake; I know my timing's bad…"

"Bad timing, she says. Ah! Your timing isn't bad, it's awful. Why did you wait until I was at the altar?"

"Well, my plan was to catch you before the ceremony started," I explain. "Then there was this rude lady at the airport who wouldn't rent me a car because my driving license was expired, but she maxed out my credit card with the stupid deposit anyway so I didn't have any money left for a cab. I took like five different trains and buses to get to Yountville, and from there the only way I could get here was on the back of a tractor filled with hay. Then bouncer guy wouldn't let me in, so I had to cook up a distraction. I sacrificed my bag, I threw it down the moat, and I ran past security. By the time I was inside, it was too late. The ceremony had already started, so it was sort of a now-or-never moment."

"You came here riding on a hay tractor?" He's trying to keep a straight face, but I can see the corners of his mouth twitch. And for the first time since I got here, hope rises in my chest.

"I did."

"You're crazy."

"I am a bit."

"And I'm crazy."

"Are you?" I ask.

He's looking at me with such intensity, I might pass out. I want to throw myself at him and hug him, kiss him. But I'm afraid I'm going to get the sit-down finger again, so I stick to my chair.

"This morning," Jake says, still looking at me with a fire burning in his eyes, "all I could think about was you. The first thought that popped into my head when I woke up wasn't *I'm getting married today*, it was *today I'm saying goodbye to Gemma forever*. I was about to throw everything to hell. But you'd refused to speak to me for three years. You didn't return any of my calls or messages—*not one*. And I've tried, Gemma, you know I've tried."

"I know," I whisper.

"So I told myself that I didn't know anything about your life today, that you were probably already married to someone else or something, and that I had to move on with my life and leave you in the past. But the moment I saw you, I knew I wasn't getting married today. The truth is, you had me at Jake…"

"I did?"

"You did. And so, yeah, I am crazy… about you. Damn

me, I'm still in love with you."

I stare at him. "You mean you're not getting married anymore?"

"No."

A huge smile takes over my face.

"Up," he says, and I get a thumb going upward this time. "Come here," he whispers.

I get so close to him our noses almost touch.

"I missed you," he says, cupping my head in his hands and burying his nose into my hair. Well, he's not going to get a red berry rush, but I hope he won't be too disgusted. "You smell so good; I've missed your smell." Yeah, he's definitely touched in the head or crazy in love with me, because no one in his right mind would think I smelled good right now.

"Gemma?" He nuzzles my neck.

"Umm?"

"Are you having a whole conversation in your head? You know I can't hear you."

"Yeah. I mean, no. I missed you too."

I pull away from him to look him in the eyes, but he holds me close. He slides one arm around my lower back, squeezing me against the solid wall of his chest, and I melt in the warmth of his embrace. I snuggle closer to him, afraid of letting go. He strokes my hair and the side of my face until his hand slips under my chin, lifting my face up toward his. Time holds still as we lock eyes, then it seems to fast forward as he presses his lips to mine in a kiss we've both waited three years to share. It feels simultaneously as if no time and an eternity have passed since our last kiss. It's all so familiar, and yet so new. This is Jake. He still loves me and we're kissing.

After five minutes or an hour, I can't tell, Jake pulls back and buries his head into my neck. “So what now? What was your grand plan after you stole the groom?”

“I didn’t plan ahead,” I confess. “I’m not very equipped, to be honest. I don’t have a car, money, or any clothes. They’re all scattered down the moat, and bouncer guy is probably feeding them to the pigs.”

Jake roars with laughter. “I forgot how crazy life could get with you. How about I take you to dinner?”

“Dinner?”

“Yeah, you have to eat, right? We can start simple and figure out the rest as we go.”

He’s more right than he knows—the last thing I ate were the tortilla chips at the airport. I could never stomach airplane meals. I’m surprised I haven’t passed out yet.

“Still talking in your head?” Jake asks.

“Yes. No. I mean, I’d love to go to dinner with you.”

He takes my hand and guides me outside the castle into a new life.

Six

Honeymoon

Saturday, June 10—Cabo San Lucas, Mexico

I pick up the bottle of complimentary champagne from the floor and take a swig. I'm with Amelia in her honeymoon suite in Mexico, and we've been sitting on the floor at the foot of the bed drinking champagne since we got here.

"He's married," I say, staring into space. "Jake's married. I can't believe it."

"I'm not married." Amelia takes the bottle from me and gulps down the bubbly as if it were water. "Gosh, I'm such a cliché," she adds when she's done drinking. "How pathetic, going on my honeymoon with my best friend after I was dumped at the altar."

"Ah, well. Technically, *you* left *him* at the altar. And at least, in this case, your best friend's just as heartbroken as you are."

"Were you really going to bust Jake's wedding?"

"Yeah, I would have. You know, if I hadn't met…"

"My ex-fiancé's mistress." Amelia finishes the phrase for me.

"Yeah, her. You really had no clue something was up with William? Not an inkling?"

"To be honest, this past year I've been so busy planning the wedding I wouldn't have noticed a pink elephant sitting in my living room, bellowing. You know what the worst part is?"

"You'll have to change your Facebook relationship status

to 'it's complicated'?"

"No." She chortles. "To tell the truth, I'm more disappointed my perfect wedding got ruined. I'm more depressed I'm no longer a bride. It's more saddening than not being William's wife. I keep thinking no one will see the butterflies released."

"Butterflies?"

"Yeah. I had this cute mint-colored birdcage filled with all-colored butterflies, and they were supposed to open the cage when we cut the cake and all the butterflies would've soared in the air above us and it would've been beautiful."

"It would have," I say pensively. "But a wedding isn't really about the butterflies. Not unless they're in your stomach."

"No. I guess not."

"Are you in love with William?"

"I don't know how to answer. I've always taken my being in love with William as a given. I haven't asked myself that question in a very long time, and now I'm too angry and too drunk to give you a reliable answer. How about you? Are you sure you're still in love with Jake?"

"Want to know what the worst part is for me?"

"You got a Brazilian wax and no one's going to see it?"

"No." I smile despite myself. "That I can answer your question in the blink of an eye with no need to think. I'm in love with Jake. I always have been."

"Oh, Gemma, I'm so sorry. You should've gone to San Francisco to stop him."

"And what, send you a text? Hi, Ames, I just met your soon-to-be-husband's mistress. Please don't marry him. Talk to you soon. Love, Gemma*?"*

"You could've called."

"Amelia, I love you, but you're getting annoying. I could never have told you over the phone William was having an affair. You would've done the same for me, so cut the crap. Plus, I'm not even sure what Jake would've said."

"You think he would've stopped the wedding?"

"I've no idea, honestly." I take the bottle from Amelia, drink, and pass it back to her. "I last saw him three years ago, and I told him to go to hell, never picking up the phone again to answer one of his calls or messages. Chances are he hates my guts."

"Jake doesn't hate your guts."

"Well, even if he doesn't hate me, he probably doesn't love me anymore. He wouldn't be marrying someone else otherwise. Crashing his wedding would've gone down in history as one crazy-Gemma moment. If I went there pouring my heart out on his wedding day, he would've told me something like..." I do an impression of Jake's voice: "'Nice to see you, Gemma, glad to see you're okay. Now, would you mind? I'm getting married here.'"

"Gosh, Gemma, that's exactly how Jake speaks."

It stings that I remember his voice and lilt so well.

"Anyway, if I'd gone to San Francisco, I would've become an anecdote for Jake and his wife to tell their grandkids." I keep speaking in mock voices. "'Grandpa Jake, do you remember that time your crazy ex-girlfriend tried to stop you from marrying Nana? What was her name?'

"'Gemma,' someone would say.

"'Right, Gemma, what happened to her, anyway?'

"'She got even crazier with old age and now she lives alone with her ten cats.'" I conclude my recital. "So yeah, having to crash your wedding saved me from making the most embarrassing move of my life. I should probably thank you, not the other way around."

Amelia laughs her head off.

"What's so funny?"

"You are. You are literally the only person who could make me laugh on a day like this."

"You can have a spot in my crazy cat house."

Amelia chortles a little longer before she's suddenly serious again.

"Gemma?"

"Mmm?"

"How are you, seriously?"

"It's as if street workers jack-hammered my chest to dig my heart out."

"That good, uh?"

"I'm having palpitations. The thought of having lost Jake forever is giving me a panic attack. I need to stop thinking about it." I take the bottle back and drown my sorrows in Dom Pérignon.

"See, I'm not having palpitations about William," Amelia says. "Just homicidal instincts…"

"Well, Jake didn't cheat on me."

"Is she beautiful?"

I don't need to ask who 'she' is. "She had nothing on you, believe me. Plus, she was as wretched as you are. William pulled a number on her too. Up until two weeks ago, she thought she was dating the perfect guy, not an engaged, cheating scum. And if it's any consolation, she's jealous you're a blonde."

"Why? How does she know? What color is her hair?"

"She's a redhead, and she stalked you on Facebook."

"Give me my phone." Amelia leans over me and grabs it from the floor. "*I* want to stalk *her* on Facebook. What was her name again?"

"Give me the phone; you're not stalking her."

"Why not? She stalked me first."

"It wouldn't do you any good."

"Why?" Amelia narrows her eyes at me. "Is she so beautiful it'd kill me?"

"No, she's not, but it's no good, anyway. Don't torture yourself."

"As if you didn't stalk Jake's fiancée."

"*Wife*. And no, I didn't."

"Really?"

"Yes, really."

"Not even a peek?"

"No."

"Why?"

"Because when I thought I was going to crash his wedding, I didn't want to give her a face, and now—well, it'd only make me cry. Imagine if she looks like Courtney Thorne-Smith in *Ally McBeal*. It'd drive me crazy to know Jake married lawyer Barbie."

"Oh."

"Why are you oh-ing me? Don't you oh me. Have you looked her up?"

"No… yes. Just a little."

"Does she look like lawyer Barbie?"

"No, not really."

"You're lying. Give me your phone, now! I want to see her."

"No, it's not a good idea." Amelia raises her arms above her head and out of my reach. I'm too drunk to stand up and snatch the phone from her.

"Let's make a pact," Amelia proposes when I stop

struggling.

"What pact?"

"I'll bear the looks of lawyer Barbie for you if you'll bear the looks of flight attendant Barbie for me. And we promise to never look them up. Never, ever. Deal?"

"Deal. I need this pact to keep my sanity."

"Gemma?"

"Yes?"

"I'm scared." She looks me in the eyes. "I haven't been on my own in forever. What's going to happen to me?"

"You're going to be heartbroken for a while. Then you're going to start dating again and have the time of your life. Until one day, you'll meet your real soul mate and you'll live happily ever after."

"What a load of crap. You hate dating!"

"It's more of a love-hate relationship."

Amelia stares at her left hand. "I used to be so annoyingly smug with my one carat resting cozily on my finger." She shakes her head. "How am I going to show my face at work? I'll be the office joke."

"Hey, come on. No one's going to laugh at you."

"Oh, they will, especially all the single ladies I used to look down on."

"Did you look down on me too?"

"Gemma, I hate to be the one breaking it to you, but you're hardly a single lady."

"Meaning?"

"Meaning men fall for you left and right like flies. It's always *you* pushing *them* away."

"And we finally understand why. No one measured up to Jake. No one ever will. I'm doomed."

"Don't worry. You're going to be heartbroken for a while.

Then you're going to start dating again and have the time of your life. Until one day, you'll meet your real soul mate and you'll live happily ever after."

I punch her on the shoulder. "That speech was for you… it doesn't apply to me."

"Why?"

"I've already met my soul mate, and I let him go. Here come the palpitations again; please, can we change the subject?"

"It gives me palpitations that I'll need a new house," Amelia sighs.

My mood instantly brightens. "Oh, that's true. You'll have to move out. It's perfect!"

"What do you mean, it's perfect? With the rates in London, I won't be able to afford a house on my own. I'm going to need roommates again. I don't want roommates! I was supposed to be starting my adult life with my husband, not looking for flat shares."

"Yes, you're going to have *a* roommate, and it's going to be awesome!"

"Are you crazy?"

"No, I'm asking you to move in with me. Naomi's sublease expires in two weeks and I'm kicking her out. I was going to live alone, but having you as a roommate is going to be so much fun!"

"Are you serious?"

"I am."

"Oh my gosh, and you have two bathrooms! I love you."

"Me too."

"Oh."

"Not the oh again. What's going on?"

"My furniture. I'd just finished redecorating the house,

and it was so beautiful. And now we'll have to sell it. My home," she wails. "Is it bad I'm more heartbroken over my new furniture than over losing William?"

"Since you can buy all the new furniture you want, I'd say it's not bad at all. Come on, we're going to have a blast living together."

"Thank goodness you're here. You saved me today, and I know how much it cost you. I'll never be able to repay you."

"Shut up, you're making me cry. Come here." I hug Amelia and she hugs me back. We cling to each other like never before. Because right now, each other's all we have.

Seven

Fumé Blanc

Saturday, June 10—Yountville, California

I take another sip of wine from my chilled glass. "This tastes wonderful!" I'm having dinner with Jake in the cutest bistro in the core of the Napa Valley. We're dining outside with a view of the sun setting over the beautiful vineyards below us. The atmosphere couldn't be more surreal.

"I'm glad to see it's not just a fancy name," Jake says.

"A fancy name? What do you mean?"

"When Robert Mondavi created the Fumé Blanc, he did it because he was sure he'd made a wonderful wine, and since Sauvignon Blanc had a bad reputation at the time, he changed the name. I was curious to try it after hearing the story. Good to know it's not just an average wine with an expensive name."

"Definitely not average. This place is too beautiful to produce average wines."

"I know. That's why I wanted to g—" Jake stops and looks at me, embarrassed.

"Get married here?" I finish the sentence for him.

He nods.

A server arrives to take our orders, interrupting the tense moment. Once he's gone, I resume the conversation.

"Should we leave the awkward topics for after the appetizers, or rip the Band-Aid?"

"I'm a doctor; my professional opinion is to rip the Band-Aid."

"Rip it is. I'm sure we both have so many questions… how about we take turns?"

"Ladies first," Jake replies with a dashing smile.

"How long have you been with…?"

"Sharon, her name's Sharon."

Oh, what a pretty name. "So, how long have you been with Sharon?"

"Two years, we've been engaged for one."

"Are you in love with her?"

"I thought I was. I wouldn't have proposed to her otherwise. But I always knew she was second best." He gives me a long stare, and my stomach does weird things in response. "I care for Sharon, and I'm sorry I just broke her heart in a horrible way. She probably hates me right now. But it was the only thing to do. It's probably better it happened today than getting a divorce later."

"So you don't—"

"I thought it was my turn now."

"Yeah, it is. Go ahead."

"Are you moving to California?"

"Oh, wow." I should've remembered that about Jake. He likes direct questions. "I haven't planned anything yet. This morning I didn't even know if I was flying here or going to Amelia's wedding instead. But as I said, I don't care where I live. I could pass the bar here. It'd take me a while—I hear it's tough in California, but why not? Would you want me to move here?"

"So you don't care about your job anymore?"

"It's not that I don't care about my job. But I've had time to put things into perspective. I'm not an idealist kid fresh out of college who thinks she'll conquer the world. I love what I do, I'm great at it, and winning a case is still better than sex sometimes."

Jake raises a skeptical eyebrow at this.

"But in the end, a job is just that: a job. A job doesn't hug you when you come home at night, a job doesn't kiss you goodnight, and a job doesn't tell you about the Fumé Blancs of the world..."

"Oh, I see, so you want me only for my wine expertise," Jake teases.

Our orders arrive, and we eat in silence for a while. When I can't stand it anymore, I look up at him.

"My turn again." I take a deep breath and fire the question I've been burning to ask for three years. "Why did you care more about your job than you did about me—about us?"

"I never cared about my career more than I did about you. I just..." He pauses and stares at the sky for a long time before focusing his gray eyes back on me. "I took you for granted. I never thought you'd leave. And when you did... I knew it was wrong to expect you'd always put my needs and my job first. I knew it was my turn to give up something. I would've left. For you, of course I would have. You never gave me that chance. You just disappeared..."

"You knew where I was."

"Yes, I knew. But you completely cutting me out of your life wasn't exactly encouraging! And... I was mad at you for leaving and never looking back."

The conversation's getting heated; I try to smooth the tones. "So, basically, we've both just been very proud and very stupid."

I smile nervously. His jaw relaxes, and he smiles back.

"You haven't answered my question," I say.

"What question?"

"Would you want me to move here?"

"No," he replies, decisively.

Oh. My heart falls into the pit of my stomach.

"It's my turn to haul my ass to where you are," Jake adds.

My heart is immediately back in my chest and pulsating at a crazy tempo. "Are you saying what I think you're saying?"

"I don't know. What do you think I'm saying?" Jake flashes me a wicked lopsided grin. It makes him look like the boy I fell in love with so many years ago. Besides my heart racing, now there's some fluttering in my belly too.

"That you're moving to London?" I ask tentatively.

He winks at me before taking a sip of wine. "The London Clinic contacted me about a research job opportunity a while ago. I didn't give it much thought at the time. But now, it feels almost like it was destiny."

"It does. It'd be so perfect! You could move in with me—I'm kicking out my roommate from hell in two weeks when her sublease expires. I've already given her notice. You could move right in." I stop abruptly and blush bright red. "If that's what you want… if it's too much, too soon." I'm babbling. "If you need some space to… I don't know. What's the recovery protocol after a broken engagement?"

Jake throws his head back and roars with laughter.

"What's so funny?"

He shakes his head. "I'd forgotten…"

"What?"

"What it's like to be around you… how cute you are… how much…" he stops.

"How much w-what?"

He looks me straight in the eyes. "How much I love you."

Eeeeeeeeee. I could die happy now. Jake's stare on me is so intense it fries my brain.

"I love you too. So, so much. I'm so sorry I've waited this long to come tell you… we wasted so much time…"

"We're not going to waste another day. I'd be happy to move in with you."

I beam at him; I've never been this happy.

"So you're not regretting your decision, not even a little?"

"No. I'm sorry for the pain I've caused…"

"Me too," I interrupt him.

"But I couldn't stay. You are who I want. You always have been…"

Unfortunately, my phone rings at this point, interrupting Jake.

"It's my sister," I say. "Do you mind if I pick up? She calls so rarely; it could be important."

"Say hello to her from me."

I mouth "thank you" and slide my finger on the screen to answer.

"Hello."

"Is it true?" my sister asks.

"And hi to you too. Is what true?"

"Did you crash Jake's wedding?"

My eyes widen. "How do you know about that?"

"Gossip travels fast. So, is it true?"

"Mmm-hmm."

She whoops so loudly I have to distance the phone from my ear.

"Are you with him now?"

"Yes."

"Wait, am I interrupting something?"

"Yes, we're having dinner."

"I'll let you get back to your dinner and report to Mom and Dad that you're fine. But call me back soon and let me know if you can spare two days to come down to San Diego since you're already in Cali. I'd love to see you."

"I'll see what I can do. My card's sort of maxed out at the moment, but the balance should refresh in a few days. Now I need to sort out what..." I peek at Jake from under my brows. "What my next steps are going to be."

"All right, I'll leave you to your *sorting*. Have fun and don't do anything I wouldn't do."

"That amounts to more or less nothing."

"That's why I said it. Bye-bye. Love yah, and Jake too."

"Same here. Bye." I end the call.

"So, where were we?" Jake asks.

"Aw, let me see... You were telling me how I was your one and only..."

A ringtone interrupts us again. It's Jake's phone this time. He takes it out of his pocket and looks at the caller ID. "It's my mom. I should probably take this. She's going to be worried sick."

He stands up and says "Hello" into the phone, then walks a few steps away—enough for me not to be able to hear what he's saying. He scratches his head as he talks to his mom. After a few minutes, he's back.

"She wants to talk to you." Jake hands me the phone as he sits down at the table.

I take it with shaking, clammy hands.

"H-hello?"

"Hello, Gemma, my dear."

"Hello, Mrs. Wilder."

"Jake's my eldest son, and he was getting married today."

"Mrs. Wilder, I'm sorry for..."

"No need to be," she cuts me off. "I always knew you were the right woman for him."

"Oh, wow. Thank you."

"But as I said, today was Jake's wedding day… Just know I expect to have grandkids sooner rather than later."

"Aw, well…" I don't know what to say.

"Have a nice evening, Gemma."

"Yeah, you too, Mrs. Wilder."

She hangs up. I stare at Jake, petrified.

"That bad?" he asks. "What did she want to tell you?"

"That she expects grandkids!"

Jake laughs again. "Poor woman, I guess today was quite a shock for her."

"What did she tell you?"

"Oh, just mundane details." He waves me off.

"Like what?"

"Like Edward's going to my house to get all my things before Sharon burns everything."

I bring my hand to my mouth. "Jake, I'm so sorry. I've ruined her life, haven't I?"

From across the table, Jake takes my hand away from my mouth and into his hands. He brushes his thumbs on my palm in soothing circles. "You didn't ruin her life. I did. I did it when I proposed to her knowing that deep in my heart she wasn't the woman I wanted. I did this, not you. In the end, it will be better for Sharon this way. Trust me."

"I feel horrible to be this happy at someone else's expense."

"This one's on me."

A server arrives with the check, and I'm grateful for the interruption.

"Where are you staying tonight?" Jake asks.

"No idea. I didn't book a hotel, I don't have any money, and the only clean clothes I have left are the ones Edward was able to salvage from the moat." Jake's brother was the one who organized our escape from the castle. He retrieved my bag, procured a car, and made sure we made our way out unseen.

Jake chuckles again.

"What about you?" I ask.

"I was supposed to be on my way to Aruba right now and my house is definitely off limits." I tense again. "But, unlike you, I have a working credit card." Jake smiles, vanishing my anxiety. "We can check into a hotel." He wiggles his eyebrows at me jokingly and I blush despite myself.

"I'm not sure I should go to a hotel with you. You look like someone with bad intentions," I say, standing up.

His eyes darken as he stands next to me. "Do I?" he says innocently.

I melt under his stare. "Let's go," I whisper.

Eight
Ashes

♦♦♦

Sunday, June 11—Cabo San Lucas, Mexico

"Make it stop," I moan, as an annoying sound makes my head pound.

"It's your phone. You make it stop," a female someone complains next to me.

I'm on the edge of a double bed with expensive, pristine white sheets, which attack my sore eyes with their brightness as I pull one eyelid open to have a look around to figure out what the hell is going on. I spy a semi-naked woman sleeping next to me. It's Amelia.

I roll over the bed, whining. Last night, drowning our pain in alcohol seemed like the best of ideas. This morning, not so much. I tumble off the bed and crawl on the floor on my hands and knees, looking for my phone while trying to keep my eyes almost completely shut, relying on my hearing instead.

I locate the phone somewhere at the foot of the bed and answer without looking at the caller ID.

"What?"

"And good morning to you too," says a voice that sounds disturbingly like my mother's, but not quite the same.

"Who's this?"

"I should be offended you don't recognize me, but by the slur in your words, I'm assuming you're drunk—or, more likely, hungover, given the time, so I forgive you. It's your dear younger sister."

"Kassandra," I whisper.

"Yep, the one and only."

"What do you want?"

"Where are you?"

"In Mexico."

"Mexico, where?"

"In a honeymoon suite somewhere."

"So it's true, you crashed Amelia's wedding?"

"Mmm-mmm."

"You two are the gossip of Chicago. How is she?"

"Blissfully sleeping and not talking to an annoying sister."

"She doesn't have a sister. Why do you sound so grumpy, anyway?"

"I'm suffering."

"More like you're wasted. Did you get drunk out of solidarity?"

"No, I have my own problems."

"What problems?"

I'm still too drunk to have brain-to-mouth filters, so I just say it.

"Jake got married yesterday."

Silence on the line. I relish the pause. By the time Kassie speaks, I'm almost asleep again.

"I'm sorry," she says.

I half-mumble, half-yawn something unintelligible.

"So you're in Mexico. You went with Amelia on her honeymoon. You're both sad, heartbroken, and drunk. I'm coming over before you two commit suicide. Give me the name of your hotel."

"I'm not giving you anything."

"Gemma Cecelia Dawson." This sounds even more like our mom.

"You're the younger sister; you don't get to Gemma-Cecelia-Dawson me."

"Yes, I do. Because the older sister's acting worse than a pubescent teen. Out with the hotel name."

"I don't remember it."

"What did we send you to Law School for? Use your brains, Gemma. Search for a towel, a pad, or something with the name of the hotel on it."

"You didn't send me to Law School. Hold on…"

I crawl back to the side of the bed, grope the nightstand for a notepad, and read the engraved name aloud,

"Las Ventanas al Paraiso, Cabo San Lucas…"

"Cabo, uh? Cool. How do you spell bentanas?"

"What did we send you to UCSD for if you can't even spell windows in Spanish?"

"You didn't send me anywhere. Okay, I've taken the name down. How long are you staying?"

"Two weeks."

"Perfect. I'll be there in two days, and I'll bring a friend."

"Wait, are you seriously coming over here? Don't you have to study or something? Isn't it too expensive?"

"I can take a break from studying. And it's not Spring Break; flights from San Diego to Cabo are pretty cheap."

"Is your friend a she?"

"Yeah, why?"

"We don't want any testosterone around. This honeymoon is a testosterone-free zone."

"See yah in two days, Gem."

"Whatever." I hang up, climb back into bed and pass out.

***

Kassandra and her friend, Lucy, fly here two days later and

they really are a breath of fresh air in our funeral party. They force us to get out of the room—they call it sun therapy, they make us eat our vegetables, they take us to visit the towns nearby, and they give us pot to smoke—they call it laughing therapy. Normally, I would censure this behavior, but if the only thing that can get me in "high spirits" is getting high, I'll cut a break on disapproval.

Kassandra's a free spirit, much more than I was in my wildest days. And I need her vitality, her energy, to pull through these first days of my new Jake-free life.

Two weeks later, on our last night at the resort, I'm having a cocktail with my sister on the patio. We're cozily settled in plush chaise lounges, gazing at the ocean.

"Thank you for coming here." I look at Kassandra. "I know I don't say it enough, but I love you."

"Aw, puh-leeease. I can take a five-star vacation anytime you need me to."

"I know, but I also know you have your life in San Diego. And you can say what you like about this not being Spring Break, but if Mom and Dad give you the same allowance they gave me in college, this must've been a stretch on your finances."

She mumbles something and hides her face in her cocktail glass.

"What's with the guilty face?" I ask her.

"Mom and Dad helped fund this trip," she confesses.

"How come?"

"I told them why you were here and they were worried."

"You told them about Amelia's wedding?"

"No." Pause. "The other wedding."

I laugh despite myself. "Gosh, you sound like *Harry Potter.*"

"Why? They had weddings in *Harry Potter*?"

"Just one, but you said the 'other wedding', like the 'other ministry.'"

"Gemma…"

"Uh?"

"You're such a nerd."

"So I get heartbroken and you get a free vacation?"

"Come on, Mom and Dad were just worried. They didn't want you to be alone."

"I wasn't alone."

"Ames was hardly going to play cheerleader. We're family, and I was a two-hour flight away from you, which doesn't happen that often lately. I miss you."

"I miss you too. You should take up my offer and come to visit me in London. It's a fun city, I promise."

"And I promise I'll come, someday. How are you, really? Can I send you back alone?"

"I'm not going to kill myself, I swear. You've done a great job; we would've been a sad party without you. I'm going to be all right."

"Can I ask you something?"

"I'm not going to like this 'something', uh?"

"If you loved him so much, why did you break up with him?"

"I was proud and stupid and didn't realize how much I needed him. Somehow I always thought I could get him back if I really wanted to."

"And in all this time you never realized how much he meant to you?"

"Not until I found out he was getting married. What can I say? Hindsight's a bitch!"

"A real bitch. I'm going to miss you tomorrow."

I hug her from across our chaise lounge.

"Now get up, old you," Kassandra says, hopping out of

the chair. "I have wild plans for our last night in paradise." She pulls me up and turns the dock station volume to only-college-kids-wouldn't-think-this-is-too-loud. We get ready inside our room, dancing, singing, drinking, and laughing.

***

I arrive in London in the early evening the next day.

"Are you sure you're going to be okay?" I ask Amelia as the chill—compared to Mexico—air outside London City Airport hits us.

"Yeah. Will said he's going to keep away from the house for at least two weeks, giving me enough time to pack."

I suspect Will's spending those two weeks in New York with Esther, but I don't say anything.

"We'll put the house on the market right away. How about you?"

"I'm going to have a quiet weekend before it's back to life as usual on Monday."

"You want to do something?"

"No, I need a couple of days by myself."

"To mourn Jake?"

I nod.

"Well, the only way to go from here is up. For the both of us." Amelia hugs me and hops into a taxi. I take the one after hers.

As I push the door of my apartment open and drop my bag to the floor, I feel like a failure. Naomi moved out while I was in Mexico, so the apartment's completely empty. I stroll into her room and take in the mess she's left behind; she didn't bother to clean. Garbage and no-longer-wanted clothes are scattered everywhere on the floor. But I'm too depressed to get angry, and anyway, I'm so glad she's out of the house that I don't care about the amount of trash she's left for me to clean.

I walk back to the kitchen and open the fridge. The only things inside it are a huge ice cream tub and some cans of diet Coke. I couldn't have hoped for anything better. I don't care that massively enlarging my derriere with ice cream probably isn't a good idea. I need comfort food. I sit on the couch and scarf down as much cookie dough as my stomach can hold. High on sugar and fats, I wander into my bedroom and take a box out from under the bed. On the lid, I've glued a picture of a jukebox. Where the word 'jukebox' should have been, a name's spelled out of letters cut from magazines: Jakebox. I know, my teenage self had a cunning sense of humor.

I take the Jakebox into the living room, put 'Since U Been Gone' by Kelly Clarkson on replay on my iPod, light a fire in the fireplace, and sit in front of it. I take a deep breath before lifting the lid of the Jakebox. My heart starts beating violently as I stare at all the mementos of my life with Jake, years' worth of memories. I'm glad I have physical things I can burn. What do teenagers who have grown up in the era of Facebook do when they break up with the love of their life, plan an assassination on Mark Zuckerberg?

On a first look inside the Jakebox, I see some solid items I can't burn, so I take the trash bin from the kitchen, bring it back to the love-bonfire, and start sorting items.

First out of the Jakebox are the tickets from our first movie night, *Kill Bill: Volume II.* Also the night of our first kiss. *Fire.*

The *Kill Bill: Volume II* DVD itself is the next item. *Bin.*

Next is a sheet of crumpled paper Jake passed me in class the first year we dated. On top, it says, "*Prom*?" Below are two choice squares, one says, "*Yes*," and the other says, "*Yes*." I marked both of them and stamped a lipstick kiss underneath. *Fire*.

Next, little plastic golden miniatures of the Little Mermaid and Prince Eric from a Happy Meal surprise. I was obsessed by the Little Mermaid miniature because I couldn't find it anywhere and Jake ate McDonald's for a month to get me one. *Bin*.

Next, a blank card sprayed with his aftershave. I made it when I moved to Boston. I remember sniffing it whenever I missed Jake. I lift it to my nose. It's faint, but Jake's aftershave's still there. *Fire*.

Next, a ton of photos. I leaf through them, scattering them on the floor. There's everything: proms, graduations, concerts, vacations, everyday life. One, in particular, catches my eye. It's my favorite picture of Jake. I took it the first night we made love. We were at his parents' cabin at the lake. It's a shot of him from the chest up. The photo's a bit dark because Jake had the sun behind him, but his face is still visible. He's shirtless and has one arm raised above his head, braced on a tree branch. He's wearing a surfer necklace, a present from me for his birthday, which he thought was super cool. He never took it off all that summer. His face is tilted to the right, and he's smiling a crooked smile. I'm not sure why I love this picture so much, but it's… it's just Jake. My Jake. He wasn't posing or anything; he'd just looked up at me calling him when I shot this and it's as if his face is lit with love, happiness, and youth. I drop the picture back on the pile on the floor, staring at it, still overwhelmed. That's when I start sobbing. Tears blind me and rain down on the pictures. Out of rage and scorn, I collect the photos in my arms and throw them all in the fire.

Next, I pick up a stone in the shape of a heart. From a vacation somewhere. I hurl it at the bin.

Next, a sheet of paper where Jake copied the lyrics of *I*

Want to Know What Love Is for me. *Fire.*

Next, a bunch of tickets: planes, movies, school dances, and concerts. Different years, different cities… still us. *Fire.*

A CD compilation Jake made me. We still used CDs, bless us. *Bin.*

A postcard of Hawaii. We promised we wouldn't go there, not until we got married and we went on our honeymoon. *Fire.*

Seashells from a day at the beach. *Bin.*

A letter. I can't open it. Jake sent it after we broke up, pouring his heart into it and begging me to take him back. I honestly don't understand how I could not have replied. Why did I let him go? Why was I so damn proud and stupid? Why? *Fire.*

A page from my old diary. Despite my better judgment, I read this one.

Dear Diary,

For the first time in my life, I'm in love. How can I tell I'm in love for sure? Because Jake asked me to come watch his soccer practice and you know I hate soccer. It's soooooo boring. But today instead of being bored out of my mind, I'm just happy. And soccer seems like the best thing in the world.

I'm happy for the way Jake's eyes search mine on the stands before anyone else after he's scored. I'm happy for the little flutter in my belly I get every time he waves at me. And I'm happy because last night Jake kissed me, and it was the best kiss ever. Not that I've kissed anyone else before, but I'm sure Jake's the best kisser in the world.

> *I love him soooooo much. I love him sooo, soooooo much. I told him last night after the kiss. And he said it back. I'm in love. We're in love. I'm soooooooooooo happy.*

Underneath there's a Gemma-loves-Jake doodle. But Kelly Clarkson is my queen, and the only thing I'm *soooooo* going to do right now is move on. *Fire.*

Next is the first rose Jake gave me, exsiccated. Can I burn this? Better not take chances. *Bin.*

Lining the bottom of the Jakebox is the wrapping paper from the first Christmas present he gave me. I can't believe I kept this. *Fire.*

That's all, folks.

I tie a couple of tight knots on the black garbage bag resting inside the bin. I run outside to throw it in the trash before I can change my mind and try to retrieve something. When I get back inside the apartment, the only thing left is the actual Jakebox. I burn the bottom first. I take the lid in my hands and trace Jake's name with my fingers and then I throw the cover in the fire too. It stays there unscathed, suspended in time for a few seconds before the letters start to blacken and blur—I'm not sure if it's due to the fire or the tears in my eyes, or both. It doesn't matter anyway because, in five minutes, it all turns to ashes.

Nine

Dinner Talk

Thursday, June 29—London

In my apartment, I cup Jake's face and kiss him. "I can't believe you're really here." It took him three weeks to settle all his things in California, pack his stuff, and join me in the U.K. Meanwhile, I went to visit my sister in San Diego and I got back to London in time to clean the mess Naomi—my former roommate from hell—had left hanging around.

"I can't wait to show you London. You're going to love it."

"Not as much as I love you." He kisses the tip of my nose.

"Were you able to bring everything?"

"I've brought the essentials, my mom's selling whatever I've left in Cali, and the rest's arriving by cargo ship next month."

"You have much? Because my place isn't that big."

"Don't worry; I won't steal your closet space."

"So, err… Sharon didn't burn anything?"

"No. She didn't."

"Did you see her?"

"I did."

"And?"

"She was tanned. She went on our honeymoon with her bridesmaids."

"That's not what I'm asking."

"She was fine, really. Hurt, but on the mend. I apologized; I owed it to her. She's very rational; she understands what happened. She said it probably saved us from divorcing in a few years."

"I wish I could apologize too."

"She's rational, not a saint. You'd better steer clear for at least twenty years."

"I feel horrible for what I did to her."

"Come here." Jake grabs me and I melt into his arms. "She'll be fine. She's going to meet the right guy for her, and when that happens, she'll be grateful to you too."

I let him soothe me. "Was your family upset you're moving here?"

"No. It's a bit farther away than San Francisco, but it's not like I was exactly living at home even before. So it's not much of a change for them. A couple more hours on a plane when they visit. That's all."

"So they don't hate me for ruining your wedding and hauling you to another continent?"

"No, definitely not. My mom was happy. She'd given me a speech about 'unresolved things' before the wedding. And I see now she was probably talking about you."

"You think?"

"I'm pretty sure. She said she knew I wasn't going to marry Sharon the moment you burst into the room, followed by security."

"Aw, gosh. Don't make me think about bouncer guy. So your family's happy about us?"

"If I'm happy, they're happy." Jake leans in and kisses me again.

After the kiss, I decide to change the subject and shake off the moping mood. "Are you jetlagged?"

"No, not too much. Why?"

"Amelia invited us to dinner at her place tomorrow night. I know you just got here and that you begin work on Monday, but I haven't seen Amelia in forever and I ditched her wedding to… well… crash yours. So it'd be great if we could go. But if you don't want to, I can tell her to rain check for next week."

"No, tomorrow's fine. I want to see Amelia; it's been ages for me too. And her husband could become a good friend."

"Are you missing California already?" I ask, worried.

"No, but I've lived there for a decade. Most of my friends are there. It's weird living in a city where I don't know anyone except you and Amelia."

"London will swipe you in like a tornado. You'll see. There are so many people here, it's impossible not to make friends."

***

The next evening we're standing in front of Amelia's door with a bottle of wine and a handful of good expectations for the night. But as William opens the door to let us in, all my optimism is crushed. William's being perfectly nice and polite. He smiles, shakes Jake's hand with an attitude of male comradeship, hugs me, offers us wine… but something's off. I can feel an emphatic wave of awkwardness coming from him. As perfect as all his gestures are, they don't feel sincere. It's as if he wishes he were anywhere but here. I'm probably over-analyzing as always and he's just tired after a week at work. Maybe tonight he wanted to stretch on the couch watching a movie instead of having to entertain guests.

"Gemma." Amelia launches herself at me and crushes me in a hug. Now, this is a heartfelt greeting. "I've missed you so much!"

"Me too. Ames, I'm so sorry I missed your wedding."

"Don't. You don't need to apologize; you had a very good reason." She lets me go and shifts her attention to Jake.

"Come here, you very good reason," she tells him. "I've missed you too." They hug. "It was about time you two came to your senses and stopped wasting your lives."

"Still bossy, are we?" Jake teases.

"As always. Please sit down; I'll bring the appetizers in a second."

As the night proceeds, I can't shake the sensation that something's off between Will and Amelia. It's nothing they do, more what they don't do. They never touch, they never kiss—and I'm not saying they should make out at the dinner table, but I expected a newly wedded couple to be at least a little overbearing in the PDA department. They never look at each other, like *at all*. I try all evening to convince myself it's just my imagination, and that I'm reading signals where there's nothing to read—at least until William drops a conversational bomb on the table.

"So Jake," he says, "would you say calling off your wedding was the best decision you could have made?"

I stare at him dumbfounded. Did he really just ask that? I look at Jake; he's taken aback by the question, but he's recovering fast.

"It was the best decision I could have made given the circumstances. I should probably have realized I was making a mistake way sooner than the day I walked down the aisle."

"Mmm," William presses him. "But even after you realised it was a mistake, didn't you feel the pressure of your family, her family, your friends?"

Why's Will insisting so much on this topic? What's he playing at? Why does he keep asking Jake about his once-was-wife-to-be? As if she wasn't enough of a skeleton in our closet already. I know Jake doesn't have any regrets, but the less he thinks about Sharon and what we did to her, the better.

"Will, maybe Jake doesn't want to discuss this particular

topic over dinner," Amelia chides her husband.

"No, it's okay," Jake says. "I guess it was the elephant in the room." I love him so much for how he owns the situation. "And to answer your question, I didn't have much time to feel the pressure. It was a split second decision. I knew what I should do, what I wanted to do, and I did it."

"T-that's admirable," William says. Then he grabs his glass of wine and downs it.

The awkwardness at the table has spiked to new heights.

"Well," Amelia says, looking mortified. "It's time to serve the main course." She gets up and starts collecting our empty salad plates.

"I'll help you," I say. I take my and Jake's plates and follow her into the kitchen. "Hey."

"Hey."

"Is everything all right?" I ask.

She stares at the sink for a while before answering. "Yes, and no. Everything seems perfect on the surface. But deep down, something's wrong."

"Is it William?"

"He's a big part, but it's not just him. It's… not right. It's hard to explain. It's like I've spent the last year on a wedding planning high. And now that my perfect wedding's over, my marriage is… I don't know."

"You don't know, as in?"

"Like yesterday, for example, I tried to think about the last real conversation I had with Will. And I can't remember one that didn't involve flowers, venues, hors d'oeuvres, or some other wedding-related thing."

"But what about the honeymoon? Did you guys have a good time?"

"It was… lovely," Amelia says in a tone between sad and spiteful. "But it wasn't passionate, or intense, or exciting. It was just mature."

"Was it you, or was it him?"

"It was the both of us. He didn't make an effort. And I couldn't be bothered to make an effort either. I'd rather read beach novels in peace by the pool than make an effort to talk to my husband. And he seemed content looking at his phone all day instead of talking to me. He seems to be attached to the thing these days. He takes it everywhere he goes, even to the bathroom. I might've become jealous of his phone."

"But was this just the honeymoon, or was it also before, after? Maybe you need to relax after all the stress of the wedding."

Amelia bites her lower lip. I read indecision in her features.

"What, honey? You can tell me."

"I've no idea how it was before. It's awful. I've spent the last year obsessing about the wedding, and with work and everything else… I didn't notice Will at all. I'm a horrible person."

"No, you're not. You guys just need some time to adjust."

"I don't know, Gem, I'm having thoughts someone who just got married shouldn't have."

"Like?"

"Like it was a huge mistake. Last night I was having drinks with my colleagues after work, and even though I can't stand half of them when the night was over, I found myself dreading coming home. I didn't want to. What does that say about me? I'm the worst wife ever."

"Come here." I hug her. "It doesn't say anything; it's not as bad as you think, I promise. You love Will. Talk to him. I'm sure you guys can fix whatever's going on with you two."

"Yeah, yeah. You're right; I'm being silly and getting too

much into my own head. Okay, let's bring the main course out or the boys will start wondering where we went."

***

"That was..." Jake pauses to find the right word. "Interesting." We're outside, walking toward the Tube to get back home. "But to be honest, I don't think William will become my new BFF."

"You didn't like him, did you?"

"The guy didn't do anything wrong per se. It was just weird."

"Definitely weird."

"What was with all those questions about canceling my wedding?"

"You mean he asked more?"

"While you girls were in the kitchen, he kept grilling me with all these personal questions. It was crazy."

"I'm so sorry. This probably wasn't the evening you had in mind, uh?"

"What did Amelia say? Is she okay?"

"No, she's not. She senses something's off too. She said she's been neglecting Will for a year to organize the wedding and she feels bad about it. She said he seems more attached to his phone than to her lately."

"Meaning?"

"She said he takes his phone everywhere he goes, even to the bathroom."

Jake lets out a low whistle.

"Why are you whistling?"

"I hate to be the one to break it to you, but when a guy is that attached to his phone, it's because he's got something to hide."

"To hide? Like what?"

Jake throws me a side stare.

"You think there's another woman?"

"I won't lie to you. From the way he kept asking me how I felt for following my heart and, I quote, 'freeing myself from the chains of family's expectations'—yeah—he was talking like a guy who wished he'd done the same thing."

"And left Amelia at the altar?"

"Or before. Or he's thinking about doing it now."

"Did he say something else?"

"Yeah, he asked if it was good to be with the girl I really loved…"

"And you don't think he was talking about Amelia?"

"Somehow, I'm pretty sure he wasn't."

"Oh gosh. And I told her everything would be fine."

"It will be. If they're not right for each other, the sooner they realize it, the better. Believe me, I talk from experience."

"I hope you're right." I stop in front of a set of steps leading underground. "This is our station. Let's go home."

Ten

Team Building

♦♦♦

Wednesday, June 28—London

It takes a lot of work to clean Naomi's mess, but it's as good a distraction as any to keep me busy on the weekend or after work. Any activity is better than no activity as my stupid heart tends to take over and voice its complaints whenever I'm idle. So I'm keeping busy and working myself to exhaustion, both at the office—taking on more cases than any one person could handle, and at home—rubbing clean every small crevice of this apartment until it shines as new.

Right now, I'm helping Amelia move her final boxes into her room. As I deposit the last cardboard box on her bed, Amelia appears on the threshold looking like a human Christmas tree of bags. She comes into her room, kicks a box out of her way with a stiletto-clad foot, and drops all the bags on top of some other boxes before collapsing on the bed.

I take a bottle of white wine out of the fridge, grab two glasses, and join her.

"Celebratory drink?" I ask, offering Amelia one of the glasses.

"What are we celebrating?"

She seems off.

"You moving in with me?"

"To moves!" She clinks her glass against mine with an undecipherable smile and takes a gulp of wine slightly too large to be healthy.

"I sense some bitter-sweetness here. What's going on?"

"William's moving to New York to be with the flight attendant."

"She took him back?"

"Apparently they're soul mates, destined to be together."

"So, are you… mmm… jealous?"

"More bitter." She takes another long sip of wine. "It doesn't seem fair that he gets to cheat on me for a year, ruin my life, and live happily ever after with his mistress. It just isn't fair."

"It isn't fair."

"No. It adds insult to injury. I'd much rather he be miserable and suffering. Am I a horrible person for wishing that?"

"No, just human."

"It's just that, at this point in my life I'm supposed to be shopping for ovulation predictor kits, not I'm-close-to-thirty-single-and-desperate shoes!"

"You bought new shoes?"

"Yep."

"Can I see them?"

"Sure." Amelia gets up and brings to the bed one of the many bags she carried into the apartment. "Here they are."

"Oh my gosh, Ames!" I take the shoes out of the box and they're the sexiest pair of black stilettos I've ever seen. They're wrap-around sandals made of a net of crystal-covered leather. The motif looks like sparkly fish scales. "These aren't I'm-single-and-desperate shoes, these are I'm-smoking-hot-and-you'd-be-lucky-to-kiss-my-toes shoes. Any special occasion?"

"Tomorrow evening I've got drinks with my colleagues. I hate those things, but they're supposed to be for team building, so I've to go. Oh, and you're coming with me."

"Am I? Why?"

"I need a friend there. There's this guy at the office. I hate him, he's worse than William."

As she says this Amelia turns purple.

"Worse than William?" I wonder what a dude could've done to be classified as worse than William, given present circumstances. He must've sunk pretty low. "What did he do?"

"He stole one of my accounts, then he made me cry, and then he kissed me." Amelia pouts and I almost choke on my wine at the kissing part.

"He kissed you?"

"Yeah, the guts of him."

I smirk; something tells me Amelia didn't exactly dislike the kiss. "Good kisser or bad kisser?"

"Good. I mean, average."

"Uh-huh. And how did you go from the client stealing to the crying to the kissing?"

"He announced the account change this morning at the staff meeting. In front of everyone, *the bastard*."

"He sounds a bit jerky. Is it office policy to steal each other's clients?"

"It's accepted. The partners think it keeps the working environment more lively."

"So he what? He waited for you to be on your honeymoon to steal one of your accounts?"

"Precisely."

"What a D-bag. But why you? Did he want to be mean to you?"

"Yes."

"Why?"

"I guess it was payback."

"Payback for what?"

"For me stealing his biggest client last month," Amelia replies, unconcerned.

"Amelia! You made it sound like he was bad, and you're worse than him."

"At least I had the class not to gloat about it in his face."

"Is that how he made you cry?"

"No, much, much worse."

I stare at her interrogatively.

"Once the meeting was over, he came into my office to gloat. He asked me if I'd liked my wedding present."

I stop mid-sip, shocked. "He didn't."

"He did."

I squeeze her knee.

"That's when I lost it. He was there, standing on my threshold all arrogant and smug, and I'd just found out Will was moving to New York… I threw the first thing I found—a mug—at him and I-I started crying. Ugly, hysterical crying. I couldn't stop myself. I kept sobbing and sobbing."

"And what did he—what's his name?—do?"

"Dylan, his name's Dylan. He came into the office and closed the door."

And the plot thickens.

"He had the nerve to ask me why I was crying. I told him that stealing my client was okay; it was fair game. But mocking me about my failed marriage, or non-wedding, wasn't cool."

"Yeah, not cool."

"Then he asked me what I meant by failed marriage. And I said he could stop pretending he didn't know. Then he asked what was it he was supposed to know. So I screamed in his face that my husband-to-be had cheated on me for a year and that my maid of honor had to tell me while I was at the altar…"

"Yep, I'm familiar with that part of the story. So what did he do then?"

"He asked me if I was married. I said, no. Then he asked me if I was engaged, or seeing someone. And I asked him if he enjoyed being a sadist, and that's when he kissed me."

"Just like that?"

"Just like that. I was yelling at him and he grabbed me by the shoulders and kissed me."

"And you?"

"At first I was so surprised I didn't know what was going on. Then, I might've kissed him back a little bit before I came to my senses, pushed him away, slapped him in the face, and threw him out of my office."

"How's this Dylan in the looks department?"

"He's okay, I guess."

"Mmm. Interesting."

"What's interesting?"

"So you hate the guy?"

"Yes, definitely hate him."

"Even if he's hot, a very good kisser, and clearly into you?"

"He's not into me."

"Why would he kiss you the moment he finds out you're not married or engaged if he's not into you?"

"Maybe it was the only thing he could think of to make me stop screaming at him. And after I slapped him, he's obviously going to hate me even more than he did before."

"Have you seen him after the kissing incident?"

"No, I steered clear of him all day."

"Mmm, I don't know. I'll have to meet him before I can

form a complete opinion. Actually, it's good you have a date with him tomorrow night. I can't wait to meet Dylan the kisser."

"It's not a date. It's office drinks."

"Yeah, and that's why you bought take-me-to-bed shoes especially for the occasion."

Amelia smothers me with a pillow.

"What are you going to wear?"

"No idea. You want to help me choose?" she asks, getting up from the bed.

"Sure." I offer my hand, and she pulls me up.

We start digging outfits out of her suitcase. I love girls' nights. And this is such a perfect one I almost don't think about Jake at all. *Almost.*

***

At six-thirty the following evening, we're pushing our way into a posh bar in central London. Amelia's wearing her new shoes and a simple-but-sexy LBD. And since last night we were going through Amelia's wardrobe, I borrowed my outfit from her closet. I'm wearing—drum roll here—a stretch-jersey print dress. A big change from my usual color palette of monochrome boring.

"Let's go to the bar, I need a drink," Amelia suggests.

"Is the kisser already here?" I ask. I can't wait to see this guy.

Amelia takes a quick scan of the room. "No, not yet."

"Drinks it is then." I take her hand and shoulder my way into the crowd.

When we finally reach the bar, I order two martinis and two shots. Amelia needs to loosen up a little. As for me, the more alcohol in me, the less I think about Jake on his honeymoon; Jake moving into his new house with his wife;

Jake making love to her… you get the gist.

"Here, shots first!" I take the two glasses and pass one to Amelia.

"I'm not doing shots. Are you crazy?"

"Why not?"

"I don't want to get drunk in front of all my colleagues. I'm already the office joke for what happened with Will. The last thing I need is to embarrass myself further."

"I'm sure no one's making fun of you for what happened."

"No? You're going to find out very soon. Flotsam and Jetsam are coming this way so you can see for yourself how charming my female colleagues are."

"You named them Flotsam and Jetsam? After the Sea Witch minions in *The Little Mermaid*?"

"Yes, Flotsam's the blonde," Amelia whispers before parting her lips in a big, fake smile. "Felicia, Jackie… you made it."

I turn around and choke on a chuckle. If Flotsam and Jetsam had to drink a magic potion and transform into deadly mean girls, Felicia and Jackie would make an excellent representation. They're two thin Prada-clad evil-smiling minions. They even have their arms intertwined just like the eels' tails in the movie, and apparently, they speak in unison too.

"Amelia, so good to see you," they say in high-pitched voices, air kissing my friend.

"And who's your friend?" Jetsam asks.

"Gemma, nice to meet you." I wave to avoid having to shake their hands.

"We were just doing shots." Amelia downs hers and I follow her lead. "You want to join us?"

"Now, Amelia. Shots? Seriously?" Flotsam asks. "Isn't it a jot juvenile?"

"But now that you're newly single," Jetsam picks up the snarky banter, "you're up for a bit of wildness."

"So you two gals are married?" I jump into the conversation.

"No, we're too concentrated on our careers," they reply in chorus.

"We don't want to keep you from your team building then," I say.

"It was so nice meeting you," Flotsam says, moving away.

"So nice," Jetsam echoes and they're gone.

I goggle my eyes at Amelia.

"Told yah. And thanks for the shot—I needed it to survive *that*."

"We can move on to less juvenile drinks." I do an impression of Flotsam's shrill voice and pass Amelia her martini. She grabs the glass and turns around so quickly, her drink sloshes on the bar.

"Hey, careful. You're spilling your drink."

"He's here," Amelia hisses.

"The kisser? Where?"

"Two tall guys at the door, he's the one on the right."

"Who, David Beckham doppelgänger in a suit?"

"He's not David Beckham's doppelgänger!"

"Mmm, I bet he wouldn't look too bad in an underwear ad."

"You're the worst. Next time, you're staying at home. What's he doing?"

"Looking around… as if he's searching for something, and… he's found it!"

"How do you know he's found it?"

"Because he's coming over here."

I watch David Beckham whisper something to his friend before moving decidedly in our direction. I turn around to face the bar as Amelia's already doing.

"What? Talk to me so he'll have to go away."

"Nope. You'll have to talk to him. And I'll be here discreetly listening to all you guys say."

"You're the worst friend ever; you were supposed to come here to…"

"Amelia?" A deep voice coming from behind us interrupts her babbling.

"Dylan," she says coldly, turning around to face him.

I make myself as small and inconspicuous as possible while I hang onto their every word.

"I wanted to talk to you about what happened yesterday."

"Good. I'm glad you came here to apologize."

"Apologize? Why should I apologize? You're the one who slapped me. *You* should apologize."

"You deserved the slap. You stole my account, you made me cry, and then you kissed me!"

"And tell me you didn't like it."

Even though I'm not watching them, I sense he's moved forward, nailing Amelia against the bar. The guy's bold. I like him.

"Of course I didn't like it." She's trying to have an indignant-professional tone, but she's achieving more of a meowing-kitten one.

"So why did you kiss me back?"

"I didn't." There's a moment of silence before Amelia crumbles. "Okay, it was an instinctive reaction. I didn't expect you to kiss me. Why did you kiss me?"

"I've wanted to kiss you since the first day you set foot inside the office."

"But you've never said anything before."

"You've never been single before."

I don't hear Amelia's comeback as I get distracted by a guy next to me.

"Hi, I'm Richard Stratton. I'm supposed to keep you entertained while my mate Dylan chats Amelia up."

I turn toward him. Rumpled dark hair, on the longish side. Dark eyes, strong jaw covered in five o'clock shadow, and his lips are parted in a wicked smile. Is every single one of Amelia's coworkers so damn sexy?

"Gemma Dawson." I give him my cocktail-free hand. "Shouldn't wingmen be more discreet? And you're late. I've already been eavesdropping on their entire conversation."

"What conversation?" Richard throws me a mischievous smile and I turn around to see that indeed Amelia isn't having a conversation anymore. Instead, she's shamelessly making out with Dylan the kisser who's living up to his name. I should probably remind her that she isn't playing seven minutes in heaven in a private closet and that she's in a very public bar with all her colleagues watching. I peek at the back of the bar and immediately spot Flotsam and Jetsam staring at the couple, stone-faced. The green of their envy makes them even more similar to their fishy counterparts. Maybe I should let Amelia have her fun.

I focus on Richard. "You're right. It seems your job here is done."

"So eager to get rid of me?"

"No, sorry. That's not what I meant. I didn't mean to be rude at all."

"And you weren't. You want another drink?"

"Yes, please. A martini."

"So how do you know Amelia?" Richard asks me after ordering our drinks.

"High school. I moved here a couple of years after her."

"What do you do?"

"I'm a lawyer. You?"

"Wow, tough. I work with Amelia, same marketing agency."

"Of course, sorry, this is supposed to be your office night. I'm the intruder. What do you do at the agency, are you in sales like Amelia?"

"No, I'm head of digital. But, really, it's a bit of everything from client management to searching new business opportunities to managing digital delivery, and I run a tight commercial ship. I work directly with Amelia from time to time."

"Oh, so you're a big shot."

"Nah, not really." He shrugs.

Good-looking, charming, *and* modest.

"What do you think of these team building nights?"

"I guess some have taken their bonding more seriously than others." He chuckles, throwing a look behind my shoulders.

"Right, I feel weird standing here while they make out. Would you mind if we moved to find a table?" I smile at Richard.

"It's going to be difficult here, but if you want, we can go somewhere else. Our friends are not going to miss us."

"Aw, well. I'm not really… I didn't mean it like that. I—uh—don't think it's a good idea. It's totally my fault, not yours."

"Did you really just give me an 'it's not you, it's me'

speech five minutes after meeting me?"

Despite the awkwardness, Richard manages to make me smile. "But it really is me and not you. I am a mess."

"How come?"

"How about we move outside *this* bar and I can tell you all about it?"

Richard smiles and shows me the way with his left arm. "After you."

***

"So you wanted to crash your ex-boyfriend's wedding," Richard says. He seems amused by my story. "But you ended up having to crash your best friend's—my colleague Amelia's—one instead. Then you went on her honeymoon with her and now you're roommates. And all of this happened when?"

"In the past three weeks," I chime in. "So you see, it really is me. I've just said goodbye to the love of my life for good and I'm not open to anything new at the moment."

"Amelia was just left at the altar and she doesn't seem to be having much trouble moving on."

"Well, it turned out Amelia hasn't been in love with her fiancé for the longest time. So you see how that might speed up things. Whereas for me, I still have a broken heart."

"And that's why you won't go out on a date with me."

"You never asked me on a date," I protest.

"But if I were to, would you really say no? Not even for a bite or a friendly drink?"

I'm saved from answering by Amelia bursting out of the bar. "There you are." She looks as flustered and in disarray as someone who's been making out in a crowded bar should. "I've been looking for you all over."

"You mean when you were pausing to breathe," I whisper

in her ear.

"Richard." She nods at him.

"Amelia, enjoying the office bonding?" he teases.

"Not funny," she mouths at him.

"Dylan, my mate." Richard greets his friend who's also joined us outside. He looks… well, there's only one way to say it: like the cat who got the cream.

"I need to go to the ladies." Amelia tugs at my arm. "We'll be back in a sec," she tells her colleagues and then drags me away.

As soon as we enter the restroom, she starts pacing around with both her hands in her hair, adding to the look of general dishevelment. "Gosh. Oh, gosh. What did I do?"

"Behaved like a horny teenager?" I offer.

"Everybody saw us."

"Yep."

"I'm never going to be able to show my face in the office again. I'll have to change jobs."

"Now, that seems a bit extreme. I'm sure office flings are pretty common."

"*Why*? Why did I do it? I don't even like the guy!"

"Actually, he's not that hard on the eye," I tease. This is the understatement of the year. Dylan's a looker and we both know it.

"You're not helping. And I wasn't talking physically. I literally can't stand the guy. I hate him. So what on earth made me do that?"

"I have three answers for you. Number one: vodka. My fault. Number two: animal instinct. Your fault."

"And number three?"

"The thin line that divides hate from love… it's an easy one to cross. But I'm told hate sex can be interesting. You should give it a try."

"You're definitely not helping. You know me, I'm not this person."

"What person?"

"The person who behaves on impulses without thinking. I've always been good, calm, squared..."

"That doesn't mean it isn't time to become round."

"Are you calling me fat?" Amelia smirks.

"No. I'm just saying the way you've been all your life is not the only way. And you definitely don't *have* to keep behaving a certain way if you don't want to. You can be whoever you want and date whomever you like."

"Easy to talk. But what about you?"

"Me?"

"Yes, you and Richard."

"Uh?"

"Well, he's not hard on the eye either."

"He's just not my type."

Amelia takes a comb out of her clutch bag and pauses in front of the mirror to tame her hair. "How come he's not your type?"

I'm about to say, "*He's not Jake*," when she anticipates me.

"And don't tell me it's because he's not Jake. I want serious reasons."

It's my turn to pace around the bathroom.

"Okay, I don't have any good reason, except that he's not Jake. But don't you see? That's more important than all the good reasons in the world. He's just not him."

Amelia turns around and takes my hands in hers. "Honey, Jake's married. He's gone. He's starting a family with someone else. You've got to let him go."

"I'm not ready."

"You're never going to be ready unless you start. And Richard's a good guy, I promise."

"Well, I've already told him all my Jake drama, so I don't think he's too keen on me right now. Plus, he'd only be a rebound. It wouldn't be fair on him."

"If you've already told him about Jake, it shouldn't be a problem."

"How come?"

"Richard's an adult." She stares in the mirror. "If you told him about Jake, he knows he's risking being a rebound and he's willing to take that chance. So, if he asks you on a date, will you say yes?"

"He's not going to ask." I don't tell Amelia I practically made it clear that I'd say no.

"What if he does?"

"What about Dylan? If he were to ask you on a date, what would you say?"

"That's a completely different matter. I can't start something with a colleague."

"It might be too late for that. So?"

Amelia nods at her reflection and puts away the comb, then looks me straight in the eyes through the mirror.

"I'll say yes to Dylan, if you say yes to Richard."

"He hasn't asked me," I repeat.

"Neither has Dylan. So do we have a deal? If they ask, we both say yes?"

I roll my eyes at her in the mirror. "Deal."

Maybe she's right. I do need to move on eventually, so why not start tonight? At the thought, my body goes through a super concentrated version of a panic attack. In five seconds, my heart skips a beat at the thought of having lost

Jake forever. Then my pulse starts racing, bringing along a blind panic that spreads from my stomach to my throat. That's when a shiver goes through me and I force myself to calm down and shake away the feeling. And with that shake, I'm finally back to normal.

As we're exiting the restroom, Flotsam and Jetsam stroll in.

"Amelia," Jetsam speaks first. "We thought you might need to freshen up."

"You really have gone on a wild spree," Flotsam sneers.

I can already see their comments putting doubts in Amelia's pretty head, so I take over. "Excuse us, ladies, but we've got to go back to our dates. You should try one of those. They're *fun*, I promise."

And with that, I push Amelia out of the door and leave Flotsam and Jetsam to stare at their outraged, obnoxious faces in the mirror.

"Oh gosh," Amelia says as we push our way back out of the bar. "I'm never going to hear the end of it. They're going to make my life at the office a nightmare. But did you see their faces?" Amelia giggles. "Totally worth it. I love you."

"And I you."

"And when we were about to despair, they came back." Richard greets us as we get outside. "Ladies, we were thinking about grabbing a bite for dinner. Would you like to join us?"

I look at Richard first, his rumpled brown hair at odds with his square jaw. An open expression on his face, a twinkle in his crinkly eyes. Why not? I need this. I need a handsome guy with an honest face. Even if it's just going to be for a night, a month, or whatever.

Before answering, I observe Dylan and he appears

hungry. He's looking at Amelia as if he'd rather have her for dinner. I giggle inwardly. "I'd love to join you for dinner," I say. "But only if we can have burgers. They're my favorites, and I'm craving one."

Richard laughs. "Burgers it is, I know just the place. It's not too far away, we can walk there."

Amelia follows the exchange, slightly taken aback, then smiles and agrees. "Yeah, I could use a burger too. Let's go."

Eleven

Hack Me

Monday, July 3—London

"Sprinkle the chicken with a generous amount of curry, then submerge it entirely in broth." I read aloud the recipe instructions.

Now that Jake's here living with me, I'm more inspired to be homely, so I'm making us a proper dinner as opposed to my usual of milk and Cheerios. I add the curry and the broth and my next step is… let it rest for half an hour. That's easy!

Fifteen minutes into the resting phase, I hear the key turn in the keyhole.

"Honey, I'm home." Jake appears on the threshold, and for one second I'm overwhelmed all over again by the fact that he's here, living with me. That we're back together. My stomach contracts with a pang of joy and I launch myself at him, kissing him senseless before he even has a chance to close the door behind him. Who knew this much happiness was possible?

As we break the kiss, I bombard him with questions. I'm so anxious for him to fit into his new life.

"How was your day? How's the research center? How are the people? Did you make any friends?"

"Whoa, can I at least get my coat off?"

"Yeah, sorry. I'm just a bit over eager."

"What's this smell? Are you cooking?"

"Yep. Chicken almond curry."

"Why, no milk and Cheerios?"

This reminds me I don't get to do "first impressions" with Jake. He knows me too well. "Not for your first evening back from work." I smile at him. "So, how was it?"

I put the plates on the kitchen bar and Jake starts setting the table without me saying anything. Just as we used to do when we lived together in college. The familiarity of it all puts a warm fuzz in my belly.

"Work was great. It actually went beyond my expectations. The research lab's cutting edge, and the funding is unbelievable. Everyone there is top notch, it's intimidating."

"Means you're top notch too." I give him the glasses. "So did you make any friends?"

"I guess one day is too early to say."

"So no one stood out?"

"No. Well, except for one that I'm pretty sure is going to stick."

"Is he a doctor?"

"No, she's a feisty little thing."

"She?"

"Yeah, she."

"Is *she* beautiful?" I'm menacing him with a wooden spoon.

"Remarkably so."

"And you're telling me this… because?"

Jake comes around the kitchen bar and ruffles my hair. "Because I love messing with you."

"And how exactly is telling me about your feisty and attractive colleague messing with me?"

"She's not a colleague."

"What then? Nurse? Patient? Admin?" I'm trying to think

of all the love stories that have ever taken place in *Grey's Anatomy* to evaluate the possible combinations. I know I shouldn't be jealous, but I can't help it. I feel more possessive of Jake than ever before. I'm not sure if it's because I'm older, or because now that I know how it feels to lose him, I don't want to go through it ever again.

"Neither."

"And where did you meet her?"

"In the parking lot."

This doesn't sound right.

"So she's not a colleague, or a nurse, or a patient. Who is she?"

"The right question would be: what is she?"

"Meaning?"

"She's a cat."

"You—horrible you." I start protesting and swatting him, both with my wooden spoon and my free hand, but he suppresses my rebellion, grabbing me by the waist and planting a playful kiss on my lips. "You had me worried there for a second."

"I told you I loved messing with you." He ruffles my hair again and leans in to give me another kiss.

"And you made friends with a cat, how?"

"When I went outside to eat my tuna sandwich lunch, she was standing there in a green patch in the parking lot just outside the hospital. I sat on a bench to eat and she followed me."

"You or the tuna sandwich?"

"Both I guess. Anyway, I patted her, and she purred. Then she started staring at me, keeping the purring going."

"And you fell victim to the purring-staring combo?"

"I did."

“Happens to the best of us. It’s impossible not to crumble under the pressure of a kitty stare. So you gave her some of your sandwich.”

“Worse. I gave her so much I had to go in and buy a new one, and I ate it in the canteen because I knew that if I went back out, I’d give her my second sandwich too.”

“You’re so cute.” My heart swells with love. What did I do to deserve this man? He’s gorgeous, a doctor, and feeds stray cats. He’s impossibly kind and very much in love with me. If this is a dream, I never want to wake up. Now that I have Jake back in my life, I could never imagine living without him. A shiver goes through me as I imagine what could have happened if I’d chosen to go to Chicago instead. How horrible and lonely would my life be right now? I shake the thought away.

“You think she’s a stray?” I ask.

“Yeah. She was so thin, she looked famished.”

“You want to bring her home?”

“I’d say yes, but what if she has kittens hidden somewhere? They’d die without their mom.”

“Then I’d better start buying meal sized bags of cat food. You’ll have to feed her every day now.”

“Do we have something she can eat tomorrow?”

“Here.” I give him a can of tuna. “This will do for tomorrow.”

“Thanks.” He takes the tuna and puts it in his work bag.

“What color is she?”

“Stark white. She’s beautiful.”

“Did you give her a name?”

“No.”

“You have to.”

“Okay. She had a regal look, so how about a queen’s

name? Victoria?"

"It doesn't sound like a kitty name."

"Marie Antoinette?"

"Nah!" I make a disgusted grimace.

"Sisi?"

"Who's that?"

"The Empress of Austria."

"Sisi… it has a good ring to it. Sisi the cat—yeah, I like it."

"Sisi it is then."

"Now, are you ready for your first homemade meal?" I ask, bringing the fuming pan to the table.

"I look at it this way: at the worst, I already work in a hospital."

"Shame on you for making fun of me."

"You always were a good tease, and this smells delicious."

"I still am a good tease. Open the wine."

"Yes, madam. But I can't have more than a glass otherwise I'm toasted in the morning."

"Who, keg-stander Jake?"

"That was nineteen-year-old Jake; this is an older model."

"Still gorgeous."

He gives me a mischievous smile.

"You know, sometimes it's weird how we're the same people, but in a different way," I say.

"You still narrow your eyes when you're trying to say something deep."

"And you still pull up the corner of your mouth whenever you're teasing me."

He pours the wine and raises his glass. "What should we toast?"

"The same people and new beginnings."

"Same people and new beginnings."

As our glasses clink, my phone rings in the background.

I take a sip of wine. "Sorry, I forgot to turn it off."

"Aren't you going to answer?"

"Nah, not during dinner. I'll check it later. It'll stop in a minute."

And it does. Only, a second later it rings again. I shift uncomfortably in my seat, worried it could be work. I don't want to go into the office on my first normal-life night with Jake.

"I don't mind you picking up," Jake says.

"But I do. If it rings a third time, I'll pick up."

It does. I get up.

"It's Amelia. I hope nothing's wrong. Ames?"

"Will's cheating on me."

"Oh, gosh. Are you sure?"

Jake raises his eyebrows at me interrogatively and I twirl my index in a *later* gesture.

"I hacked his computer, I'm pretty sure."

"What? How? With whom?"

"Some girl in New York. He's over there right now… I don't know what to do."

"You want to come over? You want me to come over?"

"Is Jake there?"

"Yes."

"Good, I need the point of view of a guy. I'll be there in twenty."

"All right, sweetheart, see you soon. Bye."

I end the call.

"Amelia's coming over. Will's cheating on her."

"I hate to say I told you so. How did she find out?"

"She hacked his computer."

"You girls want to be alone?"

"No, she said she needs a guy's perspective."

We finish our meal mostly in silence.

"What's bothering you?" Jake asks after a while.

I bite my lip. "This was our first 'new life together' night… I'm sorry it ended so soon."

"Hey, Amelia's our friend, and she needs us. Plus dinner was delicious, thank you for preparing it."

"You really liked it?"

"Cross my heart. And don't worry; we've got all the evenings in the world from now on… I'm not going anywhere."

"How do you know I want to live every moment to the fullest for fear of losing you again?"

"'Cause I feel the same. After all this time, finally being with you feels too good to be true, and I'm scared to death something horrible is going to happen. But it's not. We're here. We're together. Nothing bad is going to happen."

"You promise?"

"I promise."

The doorbell rings.

"All right, let's do this. Could you please clear the plates and pour another glass of wine? Amelia's going to need it."

***

"Read this." Amelia bangs a piece of paper on the now cleared dining table before sitting next to me.

I take the offending document—it's an email print out—and read it.

Date: Sun, July 2 at 6:07 AM
From: william.reilly@hotmail.com
To: esther.porter@gmail.com
Subject: Forgive me

Esther,

I know I'm probably the last person you want to hear from, but I couldn't stay away. I can't be without you. I've been thinking about you every day since I broke your heart. A part of my body is missing when I'm not with you. I'll never forget the first time I saw you; you were crossing the airport hall, walking briskly in your blue uniform, your flaming hair bouncing behind you. You were breathtaking. I fell in love with you from the first moment I set eyes on you. And I'm sorry for what I did to you. I'm sorry for not being able to resist you. I'm sorry for not telling you I was engaged. And, most of all, I'm sorry for not being able to follow my heart and be with you. Because that's where my heart is. In New York, with you. Not at home with a wife I never talk to. I can't live trapped in a marriage I don't want with a woman I don't love. Esther, please forgive me. I made a mistake. I chose wrong. I can't live without you, I don't want to. I need you by my side. You're the only woman I want. I'll figure it out. I messed up, but I can fix it. I will fix it. Please wait for me. I'm going to make it right. Please give me another chance.

Yours always,
William

I reread the email twice before passing the sheet of paper to Jake and looking up at Amelia.

"I really don't know what to say. How did you find this?"

"It wasn't difficult. He left his computer on stand-by. He *wanted* to be caught. This way I'm leaving him and he won't have to do the dirty work."

"Ames, I'm so sorry. When did he leave for New York?"

"Yesterday, at noon. He always leaves on Sundays so he can be in class Monday morning."

"And when did you find this?"

"Last night, but I couldn't call you right away. It was… it was… too much. The way he talks about me. A woman I don't love. Trapped in a marriage… I didn't force him to propose, it was his idea to get married. Then he saw a redhead strolling by in an airport and suddenly I'm the clingy wife."

"Did, hum. Did err… she reply to this?"

"Yes."

"Did you print her answer?"

"No need to. It was a one-liner."

I wait for Amelia to tell me the one line. I have a feeling it's nothing good.

"Her reply was, 'Are you in New York?'"

"Did he reply?"

"No, he must've called her. They're probably making up right now."

"So what are you going to do?"

"All I want to do is yell at him, and he doesn't even have the decency to be here to be yelled at."

"But how do you feel?"

"I'm mad. I'm so angry… I want to smash everything I find in my path."

"Honey, I know you must be heartbroken…"

"I'm not heartbroken."

"What do you mean you're not heartbroken?"

"I told you, I haven't had a real conversation with Will since he proposed. I've been in love with my wedding for the past year and the groom was just an accessory."

"You don't mean that."

"If I'm being honest, yes, I do mean it. I'm afraid my relationship with Will was over a long time ago, only I didn't notice. He noticed, and instead of coming forward and saying it, he chose to have an affair behind my back."

"So all you feel is anger?"

"Anger, bitterness… I'm scared. I don't have a life-plan anymore. I feel cheated of my future and stupid for not knowing something was so terribly wrong. How could I not know? How could I not see it?"

"You're not stupid." It's the first time Jake has spoken since Amelia got here. "Listen, sometimes we're our own worst enemy. We're able to tell ourselves all kind of different lies to keep our heads cozily hidden in the sand. Look at me. I told myself I wasn't in love with Gemma anymore. I was ready to marry someone else just to prove it and force myself to move on. You probably knew something was wrong, and instead of addressing the problem head-on, you subconsciously chose to shift your concentration onto the wedding planning. It's not stupid, it's human."

"So are you saying what Will did was him being human?" Amelia asks viciously.

Jake knows better than to defend William in this particular circumstance. "No, that was evil…"

He smirks. And Amelia, despite herself I can tell, cracks the first smile of the evening.

Suddenly, she gets up, fluttering her hands in the air. "Oh, but I'm not going down quietly. Oh no. I already cheated on him."

My mouth falls open. "You did?"

"You betcha."

"With whom? When? For how long?"

"Oh, nothing serious. It was just a colleague in my office this morning."

"You had sex in your office, *today*?"

"No, I didn't have *sex*. There's this guy I work with, he pity-kissed me."

"Pity-kissed? Explain."

"This guy, Dylan." She starts pacing around the table. "He's a bit of a D-bag, to be honest. Anyway, today during the general staff meeting he announced he'd stolen one of my clients."

"Is that normal?"

"Encouraged even, but that's not the thing. If you steal an account from a colleague, you do it with class. You don't gloat about it."

I have some reservations about Amelia's work ethic, but I don't voice them.

"Instead, just a few sleepless hours after I read that," she points at the incriminating email, "he came into my office and asked me if I'd liked my wedding present."

"No!"

"Yes!"

"What did you do?"

"I threw a mug at him, missed his head by an inch… and then I lost it. I started crying and screaming about cheating bastards."

"And how did you go from the mug-throwing and crying to the kissing?"

"It's a bit confused. Somehow he managed to have me tell him the whole story, then he told me my husband was an idiot and then he pity-kissed me."

"That wasn't a pity-kiss."

I look at Jake for confirmation. He shakes his head, *no*.

"Oh please, I was such a mess it had to be a pity-kiss."

"Probably more of an I'm-into-you-and-I-can't-wait-for-you-to-be-divorced kiss."

"Don't say the D-word," Amelia shrieks. "Twenty-eight and already divorced. I'm worse than Ross in *Friends*."

"I'm sure Ross was already on his second divorce by twenty-eight."

"That hardly makes it better."

"Come here." I pull her onto my lap and hug her. "You're going to be fine. We're going to get through this."

Amelia starts sobbing on my shoulder. "I'm so glad you're here."

"I'm always here for you."

"Listen, can I stay here tonight? I don't want to go back to that house."

"Of course you can stay." I throw an apologetic glance at Jake, but he's nodding his head approvingly. And in this moment, I feel even luckier he's here by my side and more in love than ever.

Twelve

Terminate

♦♦♦

Friday, July 28—London

The working week is over and I'm ready for a cozy night in watching romcoms. I'm already settled on the couch. Amelia has "plans." She didn't tell me what they are, but by the amount of time she's spent in the bathroom, I'm guessing they involve a certain David Beckham doppelgänger.

Ping.

My phone bleeps. I unlock the screen and see with a jolt that it's Richard. This is a surprise. We exchanged numbers the night we met, but I've never texted him, and up until today, he's never texted me either. After a month, I thought he wasn't going to.

I read the text.

Hey, beautiful

Hey, you

Where've u been hiding?

Been a while

Crazy couple of weeks @ work

It's as good an excuse as any.

I thought I'd say hello

What do I reply? The only thing I can think of is hello, but it seems pretty lame. I bite my lower lip, trying to decide what to write when Richard saves me by texting again.

What r u up to?

Movie night

With Amelia?

No, alone

I'm so pathetic.

Watching anything good?

No

Only bad movies for me

Define bad

Set unrealistic expectations about life

By life, you mean love?

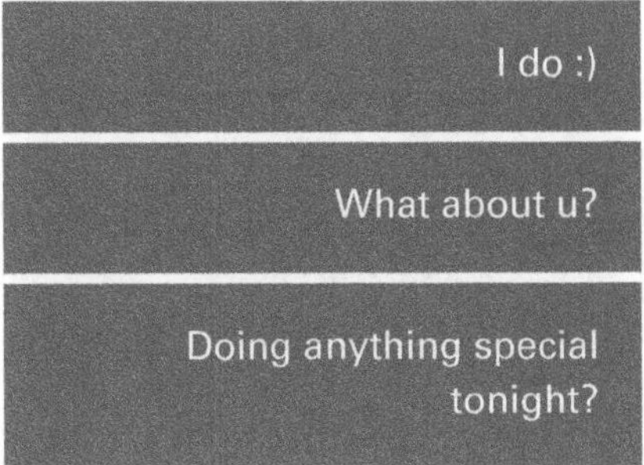

I'm distracted from the screen by Amelia appearing on the living room threshold looking devastatingly hot in an illusion-yoke lace dress. I wolf whistle at her.

"I see we've brought out the heavy artillery. What's the occasion?"

Ping.

"First official date with Dylan," Amelia says, out of breath.

"Oh, so you've finally stopped sneaking to the copy room and made it official?"

"You think I'm wrong? I'm so nervous… This is crazy. I'm crazy. He's a coworker, and it's definitely too early for me to be out there dating. I should cancel. Yeah, I should definitely cancel. This was a bad idea."

Ping.

"It wasn't a bad idea, and you didn't spend two hours getting ready to cancel. Where's the kisser taking you?"

"Stop calling him that. And I don't know, he said it was a surprise."

Ping.

"Who's sending you all these texts, anyway?" Amelia asks.

"Oh, no one."

"No one, uh? Does no one work with me, by any chance?"

"He may. Why? You know something?"

"I may. Let me see."

"No."

We both make a dive for the coffee table, but, stiletto heels notwithstanding, she's quicker in reaching the phone. Her eyes navigate the chat, and before I can stop her, she's typing.

"What are you doing? Stop typing. Give me my phone back."

I'm ready to wrestle it out of her hands when she gives it back.

"There, you're all set for the night."

I quickly read the last three messages from Richard and her reply.

I was hoping to watch bad movies with a beautiful girl

Also, I happen to be at Tesco and I've just bought popcorn

...Any ideas what I should do with it?

Why don't you come over?

"You didn't just do that. It makes me seem so forward."

"I so did. You were flirting already on your own. I just gave you a little push."

"Down the cliff. What am I going to do now?"

"I suggest you make your casual homey attire a little more casual-chic and perhaps put on a bit of makeup."

Ping.

"What does he say?" Amelia asks.

"That he'd love to come over. Did you say something about me to Richard?"

"No. He kept asking about you, and I told him that if he wanted to see you all he had to do was ask."

"And when did you decide to use my phone to have me ask him instead?"

"That was a whim."

"Now I'm screwed, and you're the worst friend ever!"

"Now, instead of a night spent moping, you have a hot date. Have fun and don't stay up too late."

She puts on her coat, grabs her bag, and exits the apartment with a wink.

Aaaarrrghhhh! I could kill her.

I rush into the bathroom and throw my pajama top on the floor, kicking it under the sink. I quickly wash my face and armpits, spray myself with deodorant, and apply some concealer and blush. In my room, I switch my sweatpants for skinny jeans and put on a super simple white blouse. I run back into the bathroom, throw my head forward and ruffle my hair with my fingers, hoping to obtain some volume. Amelia, the nerve of her! She spends two hours getting ready for her date and leaves me a twenty-minute warning at best.

The doorbell rings, interrupting my mental bashing of my best friend.

I jerk my head backward and fluff my hair to achieve a perfectly styled messy look. I check myself out in the mirror, and when I'm satisfied with my appearance, I go to open the door.

On the landing, Richard's smiling, holding a Tesco bag in one hand and a paper parcel in the other. Something smells like burgers.

Richard greets me with a smile. "I come bearing gifts."

"What gifts?"

"Oh. I was passing this little kiosk I love; they make the best burger sliders, so I thought I'd buy a few."

"You brought me burgers?" I'm already salivating. "This is *unfair* play, but I like your style." I usher him inside and hug him, feeling slightly awkward.

This is the first time I've seen him after the night we met. And even if that night was cool, we stayed solidly on just-friends territory. I had fun with him, but we didn't kiss or anything. So I feel nervous being alone in my apartment with him. Is this really a date?

I let Richard go, but not before relieving him of the burgers bag. I open it and I'm hit by a divine fragrance of grilled meat. "Can we eat them right away?"

"Sure, I'm a wise man. I wouldn't deny you burgers."

I point at the big table. "Have a seat."

I empty the bag of deliciousness onto a plate and bring two more to the table along with some paper napkins. I don't even wait to be seated before I munch on half a slider.

"So you bring burgers to all your girls or is it just me?"

"I'll admit they usually prefer roses, but with you, it seemed a safer bet."

"It was. I'd pick burgers over roses any day. And you should know I'm much more amiable on a full stomach; I haven't had dinner yet."

After dinner, Richard sags onto the couch. "So what are we watching?"

I put a bag of butter popcorn in the microwave and walk toward the TV stand. "Mmm, Amelia bought me a DVD set of eighties movies with Molly Ringwald—she's my favorite actress. So we have: *Pretty in Pink*, *Sixteen Candles*, and *The Breakfast Club*. Any preference?"

Richard smiles bravely and shrugs. "Not really."

Pop. Pop. Po-Pop. The popcorn explodes in the background.

"I'm joking. I wouldn't really subject you to Molly Ringwald night." I smile. "I'm not that evil."

"You had me there. I was scared."

"As for men friendly movies, we have Netflix or," I brush my finger over the DVD shelf, scrolling titles, "I can offer *The Terminator* collection, or we can watch something by Tarantino—I have all his movies except *Kill Bill*." 'Cause I trashed the DVD as it reminded me too much of my ex. No, Jake's a taboo thinking topic tonight. "Or there's the entire *X-Men* saga."

"Since you were set on the eighties, why not watch the first *Terminator*?"

"Great!"

When the popping ends, I put the popcorn in a huge bowl and pass it to Richard. Then, I put the DVD on, turn down the lights, and sit next to him on the couch.

I try to concentrate on the movie, but Richard's presence

beside me is too distracting. What's going to happen when the movie's over? What should I do?

I still have feelings for Jake, deep ones. I can't undo them. But if I can't be with him, and that boat has definitely sailed, why not be with Richard? I know I'm not going to fall head over heels in love with him overnight, my stupid heart won't let me. But I could give it a push. I could move on physically before I have emotionally. I've always believed it would be the other way around, but I believed in so many things that in the end weren't true.

I throw a sidelong glance at Richard—his broad shoulders, dark hair, very kissable lips. There's still a giant hole in my chest that seems to grow bigger, instead of smaller, every day. Maybe Richard could fill this hole. Or maybe I don't have the faintest clue who I am or what I need anymore. Or maybe I never knew. Or maybe I need to stop over-analyzing everything and just kiss him.

Tonight I feel stupid and reckless enough to choose the latter option.

***

The next morning Amelia walks back into the house with a smile so wide stamped on her face it makes me want to puke for sugary overflow.

"So," I smirk, thoroughly enjoying her walk of shame, "how was your date with the love maker?"

"Love maker? Seriously?"

"You told me to stop calling him the kisser, and I assume after last night you've evolved to more serious bonding." I grin. "Am I assuming correctly?"

"I don't kiss and tell."

"If you don't, I won't either."

"Wait, you kissed Richard?"

I shrug oh-so-casually. "Maybe."

"No! Tell me everything." She joins me at the kitchen table and I pass her a coffee mug.

"He arrived twenty minutes after you left and he brought me burgers."

"I knew the guy was smart."

"We ate dinner, we watched *Terminator*, and while all the Sarah Connors were being killed, I kissed him."

"You made the first move?"

"I did. But Richard didn't seem displeased about it."

"Is he a good kisser?"

"He's a wonderful kisser."

"Was it only kisses?"

"There was heat, but we stayed solidly on clothes-on ground. He sensed I wasn't one hundred percent ready yet."

"Are you seeing him again?"

"Yes, we have a date next Saturday."

"So you like him?"

"Of course I do. What's not to like? He's handsome, easy going, and he brought me burgers."

"And he kissed some sense into you, apparently."

"He did. Jake's still there in the back of my head. But at least I'm not thinking about him all the time."

Amelia rolls her eyes.

"What about you and Dylan?"

She smiles wickedly and tells me about her night of passion.

Thirteen

Lucky

Friday, July 28—London

Jake's first month in London doesn't go as smoothly as it could have. My apartment's a bit cramped with three people living in it. We step on each other's toes more often than not, and it isn't exactly the romantic love nest I'd hoped for. But I can tell Amelia's glad she isn't alone in her darkest hours. She needs us after her confrontation with Will. She needs us after meeting with the divorce lawyers—I refer her to the best divorce counselor in town. And she needs us when the house she loves and has invested in so much emotionally, is put on the market.

Lately, Amelia has been more cheerful than one would expect, given the circumstances, and she finally found a nice one-bedroom apartment to rent last week. She seems eager to move out of my apartment and move on with her life. She's already moved most of her things from her old house—which sold three days after they put it on the market—to the new apartment. Right now, I'm helping her pack her last bag of clothes in my spare room before a black cab comes to pick her up in an hour.

"Are you sure you're going to be all right on your own?" I ask her.

"Yes, I'm sure, and…"

She mumbles something unintelligible.

"What was that again?"

"I said Dylan might pop over."

"Dylan the kisser?"

"Mmm-hmm."

"I didn't know he was still in the picture."

"Well, he's been really nice to me since, you know, I threw a mug at him."

"Pottery-throwing is a sure way to a man's heart."

"Anyway, we had a drink the other night after work. And we might've kissed again," she says with a mischievous smile.

There's the reason for the positive attitude. Amelia has a crush!

"Is that the night you came home outrageously late?"

"Yep."

"And here I was worrying they were overworking you at such a stressful time. Instead, there you were making out in bars."

"Guilty as charged. And I may have kissed him at the office a couple more times too. Or a lot more times."

"Oh, gosh. You're having an office romance, this is wonderful. Just what you needed after, err…"

"You mean filing for divorce and waving my ex-husband off to New York to live happily ever after with his mistress?"

"I-I, that's not what…"

"Don't worry, it's okay. We can talk about it. I can even say the word divorcee without shivering too much."

"So this Dylan guy, are we going to meet him?" I steer the conversation away from divorce talk.

"Let me see where this goes. I'm not sure if he's a rebound fling or something more."

"You mean you could potentially see it getting serious?"

"I've no idea, but he makes me feel as if I'm a teenager again. I'm kissing him all over the office, in the halls, outside the restrooms, in the copy room. It's like making out in high school when you had to avoid being caught. It's been so exciting, and he's a breath of fresh air."

"Does he have a Facebook profile?"

"Yes, why?"

"I want to see a pic. Put a face to a name."

"Oh, all right." She takes her phone from the bed where we're folding clothes and taps happily into it. "Here, this is him." She gives me the phone.

"You pulled up David Beckham's fan page."

She takes the phone back to check. "No, this is Dylan's profile picture."

I snatch the phone from her. "You're joking!"

"I'm not."

"Well, well, well… you're in trouble."

"I might be." She blushes.

"You're making out at the office. That's so fun. Have you ever been caught?"

"Yeah, definitely."

"That's not too bad."

"It is. We were spotted by the worst office gossips ever. Flotsam and Jetsam."

"Named after the Sea Witch minions?"

"Yeah, Felicia and Jackie. Two charming ladies, you should meet them. Anyway, it's not all bad they saw us. They were giving me a hard time about the divorce."

"Were they?"

"Yeah, it was mortifying."

"So they've stopped now?"

"Yep, they're too busy spreading the news they caught me having wild sex in the copy room."

"Did they… I mean, were you?"

"No. Of course, not."

"And you don't mind?"

"It's better than divorce sneers, and," Amelia smiles a naughty smile, "Dylan might've caught them gossiping. He told them off pretty harshly. They've been quiet and subdued for a while now. I suspect they both have a crush on him."

"The more you talk about the kisser, the more I like him."

"Well, don't get your hopes up too much. I'm still not sure where it's all going."

"But have you slept with him?"

"No, not yet."

"You plan to?"

"Eventually, if things keep going. I'm a bit scared; Will's the only guy I've slept with in so many years."

"I'm sure Dylan would be more than happy to tutor you." I chuckle.

Amelia swats me playfully. "*If* he sticks."

I don't tell her, but from the way she's radiating happiness, I predict Dylan's going to go a long way.

Amelia closes the zipper on her last bag and we walk to the street corner where we wait for the black cab. When it arrives, I hug her and see her off, telling her to call me if she needs anything and to have as much fun as she can tonight, even if somehow I don't think I need to tell her—Dylan's taking care of that.

When I get back inside the house, Jake has returned from work and he's sitting, shoulders hunched forward, on the couch with a miserable air about him.

"Hey you, why the long face?" I ask, shutting the door behind me. "Is it the prospect of being alone with me again?"

He looks up at me and I see he's white as ash and has a grave expression.

“Jake, what’s going on?” I ask, worried.

“Mew.” A furry black bundle replies from his lap.

“Who’s this little guy?” I do a silly talking-with-babies voice and pick up the black kitty from Jake’s lap, bringing it close to my face. “Hello you, you’re so cute. Oh, you’re so cute.” I lower the kitten onto my lap and scratch it behind the ears. It kneads my jeans for a while, purring, then settles in my lap. “Jake, please talk to me. How come you’ve got a kitty and look so sad? What happened?”

“It’s Sisi.”

“The hospital stray cat?”

“Yes. She-she died today.”

“Oh. How?”

“Hit by a car, but I can’t be sure. She was waiting for me in her usual spot. I knew something was wrong at once because she was standing a bit lopsided and she was holding this little guy in her mouth. I crouched down to pat her, and she collapsed almost immediately. She nudged the kitten toward me with her head and she was gone.”

“Jake, I’m so sorry.”

“I don’t know why I’m so sad. Bad things happen every day at work. But the thought that she waited for me, that she trusted me with the most precious thing she had…” Jake shakes his head.

“Pets have a way of getting under our skin in such a powerful way… We’re going to take care of this little guy the way Sisi wanted.”

“You’re all right with keeping him?”

“Him? You’re a boy?”

“Mew.”

“Can he stay?” Jake repeats.

“Ah! Asking a woman if she wants to keep a kitten is like

asking kids if they'd like more toys, or…"

"I get it, I get it. You're okay with the kitten." Jake's furrow relaxes a bit, and he leans on me to pet the tiny cat.

"We should name him," I say.

"I want to call him Lucky."

"You want to call a black kitten Lucky?"

"Yes, because he *is* lucky. He's going to be the most spoiled cat in the world."

"That he is. Lucky, you like it?" I ask the kitten.

"Mew."

"I'll take that as a yes." I scratch him again. "We need to do so many things," I say, turning toward Jake. "We must accessorize the house for kitten needs and we need to find a vet…"

"Come here." Jake pulls me in a side-hug. He brushes the hair away from my forehead. "I love you, you know?"

"I love you too."

"Mew."

"Yes, and we love you too," I say to Lucky.

A warm fuzz spreads in my chest. The family's expanding already, my family with Jake.

Fourteen

After You

♦♦♦

Saturday, August 5—London

The night of our first official date, Richard picks me up in a black cab. I greet him with an embarrassed peck on the lips, blushing madly as I do. I'm a shy person. I know we've kissed already, but this is still too new for me to be completely comfortable or relaxed around him. We get in the car and Richard gives the driver an address in Peckham.

"Where are we going?"

"Since we both love eighties movies, I thought you'd enjoy another one."

"There's a movie theater showing eighties movies?"

I love how I can always discover new things about London.

"Yes, it's an open-air rooftop, actually. They're showing *The Blues Brothers* tonight. You're from Chicago, right?"

"Yes, a small town nearby. I miss Chicago sometimes and I love *The Blues Brothers*!"

"They also have a great rooftop bar, so we can have a casual dinner there too."

"Sounds amazing."

And it does turn out to be amazing. The place, the movie, the sky, the food, it's all perfect. The theater is on top of a tall building with stunning panoramic views of London's skyline, watching one of my favorite movies under the stars, is incredibly romantic. It almost feels like Richard bribed the sky to stay clear of clouds and wink down at us from a million sparkly dots.

We're seated in beach-like chairs that don't allow too much closeness, but it's all right. I'm still debating where I want tonight to end. And being too close to Richard would be distracting. Every now and then, I throw a side-glance at him, taking in all the different expressions he makes that I still don't know. The way his eyes sometimes pop in surprise or the grin pulling at his lips when he's amused but not laughing yet. He's a great guy who's taken me on a perfect first date. Any girl should call herself lucky to be with him. So why can't I stop categorizing him as plan B?

When the movie's over, Richard leads me toward the elevators and we catch an empty one. As soon as the doors close, Richard's lips are on mine. He presses me against the elevator's back and lets go of me only seconds before the doors open again on the main floor. Well, he's definitely not shy. I walk outside, confused, and follow him onto the street where we jump into another black cab.

On the taxi ride home, I've as much buzzing in my belly as in my brain. My lips are still swollen from the kiss, spreading tingles of excitement through me, but the excitement is verging on panic. I have so many questions fluttering in my brain. Like, when we get home should I invite Richard in? Am I ready for third base? Will I ever be ready? Is sex third base or is there a fourth? I always get confused by the bases.

All this second-guessing is weird because I've already been with another man after Jake. His name was Michael, and we dated for a year. So it's not as if sleeping with Richard will be my first time with someone else after I broke up with Jake. Then why does it feel that way? Maybe because last time I'd deluded myself I was over Jake, whereas now I'm painfully aware that no matter how much time has passed, I'm still in love with him.

Richard chooses this moment to brush a thumb over my

hand and all my rational thinking gets sidetracked. It feels, mmm, I'm… conflicted. This is one of those classic situations where body and mind—or heart in this case—don't agree. Okay, let's calm down and put the jigsaw pieces together.

Evidence number one: *I'm in love with Jake.*

Evidence number one-b: *Jake's married to another woman and probably making love to her right at this moment.*

Evidence number two: *Richard's a great kisser, he knows what he's doing, and there's chemistry between us.*

Evidence number two-b: *I don't need to be already in love with him to sleep with him. I need to let myself fall in love with him one small step at a time. Rome wasn't built in a day.*

Evidence number three: *I'm not committing to anything for life. It's just one night. Yeah, I should take things on a day-by-day basis from now on. That should be my new life mantra.*

Final piece of evidence: *Amelia's staying at Dylan's tonight and we could have the apartment all to ourselves.*

When the black cab pulls up in front of my building, Richard asks the driver to wait for a second while he says goodbye. Ever the gentleman. I exit the car, chanting in my head over and over again:

To invite him in, or not to invite him in? To invite him in, or not to invite him in?

Richard rounds the car and is at my side in a few quick steps.

To invite him in, or not to invite him in?

"I guess this is goodnight." He cups my head with both hands and gives me the softest kiss.

To invite him in, or not to invite him in?

"I should get going now; want to do something next week?"

To invite him in, or not to invite him in?

"I… yes, I mean. Wait here."

Acting braver than I feel, I walk past Richard, lean forward, and knock on the cab's window. The driver immediately rolls it down.

"Yes, miss?"

"You can go," I tell him.

"You still need to pay me."

"Aw, oh. Yes, sure. Of course…" Why do I always make a fool of myself? I'm fumbling desperately in my purse to find my credit card when Richard pulls out a bill and passes it to the driver through the open window. The driver takes it and zooms away into the night.

"Thanks," I mumble.

He smiles. "You're welcome."

What do I do now? My split-second bravado is already gone.

"So," Richard says.

"So what?"

"You tell me." He chuckles. "You're the one who sent my taxi away."

"I did. Well, I guess now I can't leave you here alone in the street."

"That would be truly cold-hearted."

I take a deep breath. "Would you like to come in?"

"I'd love to."

I smile. "Great."

Move on, I say to myself, *you need to move on*. My new life begins tonight.

Fifteen

Our First Date

Twelve years before—Chicago area

Gemma placed a black top dangling from its hanger against her chest and stared at her reflection in the mirror. "Black top…" She paused to switch hanger. "Or pink one?"

Amelia, head resting on her hands while she lay on Gemma's bed, scrunched her pretty face at her friend before providing an answer. "The black top makes you look more sophisticated."

"I don't care about sophistication. I want to know what top will get Jake to kiss me."

"You think he's going to kiss you tonight?"

"I thought he was going to kiss me the other night, but he didn't. So what do I know?"

"But last week it wasn't a real date. You just had a walk and sat on a blanket for a while."

"And what's more romantic than sitting by the river stargazing? I still don't know why he didn't kiss me. You think he likes me?"

"Of course he likes you. He wouldn't have asked you on a real date otherwise."

"You're right, this is our official first date. I'm so nervous…"

"Why? I wish I were about to be kissed!" Amelia said, rolling on her back, her gaze lost on the ceiling, daydreaming.

"You would be if you'd agreed to go out with Teddy Parker."

"I don't like Teddy Parker. I want to date Brian."

"But he's dating Priscilla Walsh."

"The hag! I hate her. But I've heard they might break up soon. I want my first kiss to be with Brian."

"Okay, but let's worry about my first kiss for now. Pink or black?"

"Mmm... pink. It makes you less intimidating, more approachable. Utterly kissable."

Gemma put the black V-neck back in the wardrobe and pulled the pink crop top over her head. It left the hint of her belly button visible above the waistband of her high waist jeans.

"I'm pulling my hair up." Gemma used a matching pink band to tie her hair. "Strawberry lipstick. Aaand... I'm ready to be kissed." She turned toward Amelia, who jumped off the bed squealing and crushed her in a bone-tight hug.

"You have to go now," Gemma said. "Before Jake gets here."

"I'm stealing my dad's pager. Page me when you get back. I'll sneak out and come back here so you can tell me everything."

"I will."

Gemma waited in her room for the bell to ring. She had to keep drying the sweat from her palms on her jeans. What if Jake wanted to hold hands? She couldn't have sticky palms. She put an extra packet of tissues in her purse just in case. That's when the doorbell rang. Gemma braced half her body against her room's doorframe to listen to what was going on downstairs.

Her father's voice drifted up the stairs as he asked Jake to join him on the porch for a quick chat. Oh gosh, her dad was giving Jake the you-are-dating-my-daughter-be-good speech. Gemma covered her face with her hands, hoping it'd be over soon. She waited five minutes before hopping down the stairs to join them on the porch. As expected, her dad was sporting his most intimidating scowl. Jake's face was ashen, but his features were set on brave and determined. He looked so handsome in his football jacket.

"Hi." Gemma's eyes sparkled as they met with Jake's. "Can we go, Dad?"

"I want her home by eleven, not a minute later," Mr. Dawson said, still scowling at Jake.

"Yes, sir. We won't be late."

As they walked toward Mrs. Wilder's car, Gemma could feel her father's eyes still on them. Jake opened the passenger door for her, and she waited for him to get in the car with her before she spoke.

"Sorry about my dad. What did he say to you?"

"He—mmm, we're cool."

"Oh, okay. It's great your mom let you borrow the car."

"Yeah. By the way, if she asks, we went to see Harry Potter."

"Okay—yeah, my dad wouldn't be too happy about us watching Tarantino either. He doesn't know I've seen the first Kill Bill. I still want to see Harry Potter, though. We could go another time." At that instant, Gemma realized Jake hadn't yet asked her on a second date. "I mean, not that we have to go together."

"I'd love to go with you." Jake placed a hand on her knee, sending Gemma's nervous system into overdrive.

***

"For a moment there I thought she was going to forgive Bill," Gemma said as they walked back to the movie theater's parking lot.

"Nah. After all, the movie's called Kill Bill."

"You're right."

Jake opened the car door for her again and Gemma

slipped in. They didn't say much on the way home. Gemma's palms kept getting sweatier and sweatier. The date had been perfect. Jake had bought her popcorn, and halfway through the movie, he'd wrapped one arm around her shoulders. But still no kiss.

Jake took a right turn, and Gemma wrinkled her nose. "We need to go left."

"I'm not taking you home. Not yet."

Gemma's belly fluttered. "Oh."

Jake pulled up in a parking lot overlooking Lake Michigan. The view was spectacular, and Gemma's palms were the clammiest of the entire night. Jake killed the engine and turned to look at her. This was it. He was going to kiss her. Gemma watched Jake lean in closer to her with a pounding heart, unable to move, paralyzed with both fear and anticipation. Jake's lips pressed onto hers and all her worries melted as a warm fuzz spread in her chest and belly. Jake's kiss was tentative at first, soft and sweet. Until his hand wrapped around the nape of her neck, pulling her in closer, and suddenly they were kissing for real. Gemma felt her breath catch in her throat, her chest aching with how much she loved Jake. She pulled back to look at him.

He frowned. "Did I do something wrong?"

"No, it was perfect. Jake Wilder, I-I love you."

Jake's eyes widened before a smile spread on his lips. "I love you too, Gemma Dawson."

Then they were kissing again, and Gemma found herself hoping eleven o'clock would never arrive.

♥♥♥

Saturday, August 5—London

"Didn't I just kick you out of this house a week ago?" I ask Amelia.

"You did."

"So what are you doing here?"

"I'm dressing you."

I look in the bedroom mirror, perplexed. "Tell me again why I'm wearing this?"

Amelia rolls her eyes at me. "I've told you. I bought these on a whim, changed my mind, and asked for a refund. But they won't take the clothes back at the store. So, I thought they'd fit you better."

"They're like a present for me?"

"More a hand-me-down. What do you think?"

She gave me a nice pair of high waist jeans and a silky blush top to wear. "A bit retro, but I like it."

"Now pull your hair up."

I obediently scrunch my hair up into a messy bun.

"No, no. Let me do it." Amelia takes control of my head. Brushing, tugging, and finally tying my hair in a high ponytail. "Perfect. Now close your eyes." She's smiling too much; something's going on here.

I narrow my eyes at her. "Why?"

"Trust me."

I do as she says and let her pull me by the hands around the apartment. I'm familiar with the geometry of the place enough to orient myself. She's pulling me out of the bedroom, along the hall, and across the living room to the front door. A brush of cool air hits me when she opens it to drag me outside.

"You can open your eyes now."

I do. Jake's waiting outside the house, propped up against a car wearing his old high school football jacket. He's beaming at me and my mind swirls a little with the strongest sense of déjà vu.

I turn from Jake to Amelia. "What is this?"

She squeezes my shoulders. "I'm going to play with

Lucky for a bit and I'll let myself out. Have fun." She winks and disappears back inside the house.

I hop down the few steps to the curb where Jake's standing.

"So?"

"Gemma Dawson, will you go on a date with me?"

"A date?"

"Yes. I haven't taken you on a real date since we got back together."

He's right. We went to a restaurant after I crashed his wedding, and we went to that horrible dinner at Amelia's house before she found out Will was cheating on her. But those hardly qualify as dates. Then Amelia moved in with us, and we haven't had much alone time since.

"Where did the car come from?"

"I rented it."

"Are you sure you can drive on the left side?"

"We're going to find out very soon."

"And why the fuss from Amelia about these?" I flick my hands over the clothes she's made me wear. "And why the football jacket?"

Jake smiles a wicked smile. "Because I'm taking you to watch *Kill Bill*."

Kill Bill. Our first date. Our first kiss. Our first I love you. My heart wants to explode with the same aching love of that night so many years ago. I squeal and throw my hands around his neck to kiss him, but he pushes me back.

"Now, now. That will have to wait until the end of the night. We're doing things properly here."

"All right, Mr. Wilder. You're the boss."

I give him my hand and let him walk me to the other side of the car and open the passenger door for me. I slip inside and a stupidly happy smile spreads across my lips.

Six Months Later

Sixteen

Something Special

♦♦♦

Friday, March 2—London

Up for something special tonight?

It's Richard.

Special, uh?

Like what...?

It's a surprise

I'll pick you up at seven

I didn't say yes

But now you have no choice

'Cause you're too curious to say no

You know that's going to make me die of curiosity

I know

I'm evil like that!

Yes, you are

See you tonight, x

Something special, uh? I wonder what it could be. After six months of dating, Richard and I are in a good place. We have an easy, uncomplicated relationship with no drama whatsoever. We're in love and it's great. I never thought I'd say, "I love you," to anyone after Jake, but Richard made it so easy for me to fall for him.

I spend half of the day imagining what this big surprise is going to be. So far, Richard hasn't been the surprise-type. I check the calendar, but I haven't forgotten my birthday or his birthday. It's just a regular Friday night, nothing special about it. So what's up with him?

When I get home, Amelia's waiting for me with a keen expression on her face.

"How was your day, honey?" she asks.

I shrug. "Mostly like any other."

"Oh, it's going to get better."

"What do you mean?" Why are people talking in riddles today?

"There was a delivery for you."

"Where is it?"

"In your room."

I dash into my room. An amazing dress is draped on my bed with a Post-it note on it that says, "*Wear me.*" Next to it, there's a dock station with another Post-it saying, "*Play me.*" This is a surprise date version of *Alice in Wonderland.* What are we celebrating, my Very Merry Unbirthday? I wonder if a white rabbit with a ticking clock is going to make an appearance soon to tell me I'm late, which I kind of am considering it's already six. Well, at least I won't have problems choosing what to wear. I'm intrigued. Where's Richard going with this?

I push play on the dock station and it's *The Blues Brothers* soundtrack. I smile, thinking back on our first date at the film club.

To the sound of 'Everybody Needs Somebody To Love', I hop in the shower while dancing and singing like a maniac. I'll give it to Richard: he knows how to set the right atmosphere.

I quickly blow-dry my hair and step back into the room. Now, 'Do You Love Me?' is on and I can't help but shake my booty to the melody.

"Having fun?" Amelia asks, leaning against the doorframe.

"Much. Did you see this dress?" I slip it on. "It's a dream." It's a navy midi-length dress with a see-through hem and shoulder straps. It has blue floral appliques and beads all over. It's gorgeous. "My blue suede pumps will look great with it."

"Yeah, I think that was the idea."

I twirl in front of the mirror, excited. "What do you say, hair up or down?"

"Up, but loose. If you give me a comb, a hair band and

ten bobby pins I can pull the perfect bun off in five minutes."

"Yes, madam."

I give her everything she asked for. Amelia starts by backcombing the base of my hair, then pulls the back half in a side ponytail that she transforms into a side bun, and finally, zip-zap, she pins the rest of the hair on the bun in a perfectly-messy fashion. As promised, I'm red carpet ready in five minutes.

"Wow! This is super. Thank you, Ames."

"You're gorgeous."

I put eyeliner on, a generous quantity of mascara, blush, and lip-gloss, so that when the bell rings, I'm just about ready.

I shut off the dock station. "I'm going."

"Have a great night."

"I will."

"And be home by midnight," Amelia yells jokingly after me. "Or, don't come back at all."

Outside, Richard's waiting for me next to a black cab, wearing a tux. He looks dashing. As I throw my arms around his neck to kiss him, he hands me a white rose.

"You're beautiful."

"Thank you." I take the rose and smell it. "You're not too bad yourself."

"Shall we go?"

As I step into the cab, nerves attack me. Richard has gone to a lot of trouble to organize this night and I have a feeling the surprises aren't over yet. Suddenly, a horrible thought pops into my mind. He wants to ask me to move in with him. Dylan asked Amelia a while ago and she's moving out of my apartment soon. But Richard and I are definitely not ready for such a big step; we've been dating for as long as they have, but it's been casual dating, nothing too serious. I throw a side-glance at him and he smiles.

"Where are we going?" I ask.

"Be patient, we're going to get there soon."

"Haven't I suffered enough?"

He buffets my nose with a finger. "Poor you, look at the state of you," he mocks me.

"Okay, I've definitely had worse days. But you know how curious I am."

The cab stops in front of The Dorchester.

Richard gives me his hand to help me out of the cab.

"You're joking," I say as I stare at the building. "This is the most expensive restaurant in London."

"It's a special night; it called for a special place."

"What's so special about tonight?" I ask, the nagging worry poking again at my stomach. This whole thing is screaming serious relationship, commitment, moving in together. And I'm definitely not ready for all of that. Not yet.

"I got a promotion today; I wanted to celebrate with you."

So this is it. We're celebrating his promotion. I relax at once. Oh, Richard. He has style.

The restaurant's amazing, dinner's amazing, and Richard's amazing. We eat a seven-course meal with wine pairing, and by the end of the night, I'm more than a little tipsy. My head's spinning a bit, so when Richard suddenly gets incredibly serious, I don't immediately grasp the meaning of what he's saying.

"…these have been the best six months of my life. I love you so much, Gemma, I couldn't contemplate spending a day away from you."

I nod my head in assent. This is all very nice. A bit over-dramatic, maybe. But hey, who am I to complain?

"And this is why I want to make sure I don't… have to spend a single day away from you."

I keep nodding. Where's he going with this speech? And why is he being so melodramatic? The penny drops when he gets up, rounds the table, and drops to one knee.

Oh gosh! No, this isn't happening. Panic clutches my throat and my head starts spinning, for real this time. The entire room is swaying around me. I'm going to be sick. What's Richard doing on one knee? Well, there aren't many things a guy in a tux would do down on one knee in a Michelin-starred restaurant. The other patrons gasp, and the entire room stops to watch us.

I stare at Richard in horror. Is he really doing this? I watch in slow motion as he picks a blue velvet box out of his jacket pocket and opens it. Inside, there's a ring.

"Gemma Dawson, will you marry me?"

I smile a nervous smile; tears prickle my eyes. Not because I'm overwhelmed by joy, but because now I'll have to break up with him. I can't marry him. Where did he get the idea that we're marriage-ready at this point in our relationship? We've never even glossed over the topic. Tears stream down my cheeks. I try to speak, but I'm choked with emotions and I can't.

"Look how happy she is," a woman nearby says. "She can't speak."

If only you knew why, lady.

As I try to speak again, the crowd starts clapping and cheering in support. I look at Richard, his eyes warm with love, his forehead dotted with pearly beads of sweat, and his lips parted in a hopeful smile. I can't break his heart. I just can't.

"Yes, I'll marry you," I hear my voice say.

Richard slides a beautiful solitaire onto my finger and suddenly my hand feels heavier than it has ever been before.

Seventeen

Floating Memories

♥♥♥

Friday, March 2—London

"Oh, you're home already." I greet Jake with a kiss. "And you're cooking?" The apartment smells of grilled meat.

Jake looks super cute in my pink 'all about that bake' apron. (Not that I actually bake, it was a present.)

"I'm making burgers," he says.

"What's the occasion?" I ask him, immediately afraid I've forgotten something important. I'm not the best with dates, anniversaries. Since the rise of smartphones, I manage birthdays well enough, but that's about it.

"Oh, nothing special." Jake comes over to take off my coat and guides me to the table. "Wine?"

"Sure."

He pours me a glass.

"Mmm, this is good. What is it?"

"I thought you'd recognize it."

"Should I?"

"It's Fumé Blanc."

"From Napa?"

"Meow." Lucky comes brushing at my legs.

I put the wine glass back on the table and pick Lucky up. "Oh, and you had a makeover too." He's wearing a new red collar with a red bow tied to the top. "You look handsome."

"Prrr, mrrr."

"Are you sure nothing's up?" I ask Jake.

"I'm just in the mood to celebrate. Now sit down, dinner's

ready."

One bottle of Fumé Blanc and one delicious burger later, Jake seems to edge on nervous rather than full and pleasantly tipsy like myself.

"Are you going to tell me what's going on now?" I ask.

Jake gets up. "Come with me." He grabs my hands to pull me up. "I have a surprise."

He drags me to the spare bedroom and opens the door. I walk inside. The room's filled with floating red and pearl white party balloons.

"Jake, what's this?"

He smiles. "Have a look around."

I take a few tentative steps inside the room, noticing various objects dangling from most of the balloon ribbons. I grab one, and immediately, a furious blush spreads across my cheeks. I cover my face with my hands and press it against Jake's chest to hide.

"Oh, gosh. You've found the Jakebox!"

"I had a tip-off."

"I'm going to strangle that sorry excuse for a best friend. You were never supposed to find it."

"Why not? It's super cute. And I've added some things of my own."

"You did?" I peep at him from between my fingers.

"Come on, you should own the Jakebox." He spins me round and pushes me gently into the room.

I navigate the balloon maze and each one's a surprise. A million pictures of us stare back at me, some from the Jakebox and others not. They range from age fifteen up to last week. I find tickets from movie nights, concerts, vacations.

On the next balloon, I recognize a sheet of crumpled

paper Jake passed me in class the first year we started dating. On top, it says, "*Prom*?" Below are two option-squares, one says, "*Yes*," and the other says, "*Yes*." I marked both of them and stamped a lipstick kiss underneath.

"You were already such a charmer," I say.

Next, I find a page from my diary.

"Oh, you didn't read this!"

"I *soooooo* did."

I keep moving through the balloons. I find some Post-its. I used to leave them on the bathroom mirror of his house before I left in the years we were living apart. "You kept these!"

"These were my lifeline. I hated being away from you so much, especially knowing it was my fault."

"It wasn't your fault. I know I blamed you, but I shouldn't have."

"But if I'd followed you to Boston…"

"You would've hated it. And who knows where we'd be now." I turn around. "The important thing is that we're here, now." I kiss him.

"Ouch." Jake pulls back as Lucky starts climbing on his leg to try to get to the balloon ribbons.

"Someone wants to play," I say.

"He already *helped* enough with the setting up." Jake drops Lucky to the floor where he stares intently at the ribbons, one paw stretched forward menacingly.

"I bet he did."

I scratch him behind the ears and keep walking through the hidden treasures of our past. Some of the heavier items need three of four balloons to keep them afloat. Like a heart-shaped stone we picked up at the beach, or a small bag filled with seashells, and even two golden miniatures of the Little

Mermaid from McDonald's Happy Meals. And a vial filled with sand.

"Where's this from?"

"The lake. My parents' cabin."

I blush.

"Remember that day?" Jake takes hold of two pictures and shows them to me.

They're from the day we lost our virginity together. "Of course." One is my favorite pic of him. Shirtless, he has one arm raised above his head, braced on a tree branch. He's wearing a surfer necklace, which he wouldn't take off for the whole summer. The other pic is of me. I'm not staring at the camera, but at the lake. The sun's shining through my hair as if I were radiating happiness and love. Which I was.

"I don't remember this picture," I say, looking at it.

"I had this one. It's my favorite of you."

"And this is my favorite of you," I say, pointing at the other picture. "Remember that necklace I gave you? You never took it off."

"Wait, it should be here somewhere." Jake shuffles some balloons around and finds it.

"You should put it on." I take it from him and tie it around his neck. He gives me that same crooked grin, and I'm so full of love, so full of life I might explode.

Toward the end of the room, I spot a postcard of a beach in Hawaii. Where we promised we'd go for our honeymoon. My heart rate accelerates.

As I reach the very end of the room, a particularly thick cluster of balloons stands out. My heart jumps into my throat as I notice they're holding a small jewelry box. Dangling below it, there's a sheet of paper. I snatch it. It says, "*Marry me*?" Below are two option-squares; one says, "*Yes*," and the other says, "*Yes*." I look up from the sheet of paper to find Jake has detached the tiny box and is on one knee in front of me with it open. Tears fill my eyes.

"Will you…"

His words are cut off by me barreling into his arms. "Yes! Yes, yes, yes, yes!"

As I kneel on the floor in front of him, he takes the ring, a breathtaking square sapphire with a diamond halo, out of the box and slides it on my finger. An electrical tingle sparkles where his skin touches mine and my left hand feels so light it could be made of air.

We lock eyes. "I love you. I want to spend my life with you and fill the Jakebox with so many more memories."

I smile and cry at the same time. "I love you so much, I don't even know how to say it."

"Then you shouldn't talk." Jake kisses me and I melt in his arms. We make love on the floor with the same passion, the same frenzy, and the same love as our first time.

Eighteen

Lattes and Rings

♦♦♦

Saturday, March 3—London

The day after proposal-gate, I leave Richard's house as soon as I can without appearing too ungrateful, saying I want to share the good news with my friends and family and feeling like an impostor all along. I ask Amelia to meet me at a Starbucks near our house, hoping that coffee and my best friend will help me find a solution. *A way out*, my treacherous brain thinks. So here I am sharing the 'good' news over lattes.

"So what is the big announcement you had to drag me out of bed on a Saturday for?" Amelia isn't a morning person; Dylan's trying to change that.

"Richard proposed," I say flatly.

"Aw," she squeaks. "That's wonderful, amazing. I can already picture him looking dashing in a tux, and you glowing in your white gown. Let me see the ring."

She grabs my left hand, but the ring isn't there. I took it off the moment I left Richard's house.

"Why aren't you wearing it? Was it too big? You need to re-size it?"

"No, it fits me just fine. Here it is." I take it out from an inside pocket in my bag.

"This is beautiful." Amelia looks at the ring, then at my face. "Wait, if it fits, why aren't you wearing it?"

"I was afraid of losing it," I lie.

"It's not any safer in your bag. Put it on."

I do and stare at my hand questioningly.

"Why aren't you giddy with happiness?" Amelia asks. "You said yes, didn't you?"

"Mmm-mmm."

"So, what's wrong?"

"It was an ambush. I was forced to say yes."

A girl sitting next to us scoffs. We turn toward her, but she's steadily looking at her iPad and not at us, so we go back to our conversation.

"What do you mean you were forced to say yes?" Amelia is giving me a no-crap look. "Nobody held a gun to your head, I'm sure."

"Amelia, he asked me in a room full of people after the most romantic night ever. How could I have said no? I was cornered, I panicked!"

"So you said yes out of politeness?"

"At first I couldn't speak, I was too shocked. I wanted to say no. I wanted to ask him, 'What the hell? We never even discussed moving in together, what made you think I was ready for marriage?' But Richard was looking at me as if I were the most beautiful thing in the world, with his eyes full of love, and I just couldn't say no. I couldn't break his heart."

"Because you love him. You're just freaked out by the marriage thing."

"I care about Richard, he's wonderful. But I never thought about him as The One, the love of my life, Mr. Right. Call it what you like. I mean, who proposes after six months?"

The girl next to us lets out an even louder snort. I can't ignore it this time.

"Excuse me, you have a problem?"

"Actually, yes, I do." She stops pretending to be watching

her iPad and turns toward us. "Do you have any idea how rare it is to have a bloke ask you to marry him these days?"

"Err, no."

"No, exactly, you don't. All guys want to do nowadays is to Tinder you one night and never see you again. And honestly, having to sit here and listen to you complain about your—according to her," she points at Amelia, "dashing boyfriend proposing after the—according to you," she points back at me, "most perfect romantic night, is boggling my mind."

"Nobody asked you to listen in to our conversation," I point out.

"Hard not to when you're babbling aloud two feet away from me. You've ruined my breakfast. Are you happy?" She gets up and storms out of the coffee shop.

I stare at Amelia at a loss for words.

"What was that about?" she asks.

"No idea. You should introduce her to Flotsam and Jetsam, they'd make a beautiful trio."

"She did have a point, though."

"What point?"

"Any girl would be happy, ecstatic, her boyfriend proposed."

"Even after only six months?"

"Yes. What's holding you back?"

I bite my lower lip.

Amelia throws me a warning stare. "If you're about to bring Jake into this, I'm going to scream and get out of here."

"Says the one who was getting married out of inertia instead of love."

Hurt appears on Amelia's face. That was a low blow.

"I'm sorry." I backtrack immediately. "I didn't mean it

like that."

She nods her understanding.

"But I have a serious problem here," I add. "I thought you would've understood, seeing as how you almost married the wrong guy."

"William was the wrong man for me because we weren't in love with each other anymore, not because I was chasing after a ghost of my past. I thought you had closed that door."

"I have."

"Have you? Honey, Jake's gone. He's married to someone else."

"Do you have to keep rubbing it in my face?"

"Apparently, yes, as you seem inclined to overlook the fact."

"What fact?"

"That Jake *is* married. You think marrying Richard would put an end to any remote possibility you might have of getting back with Jake one day. But let me tell you, that train has departed."

"That's not… it's not like that. I have many other reasons to question this decision."

"What reasons?"

"That it's too soon. That Richard and I don't know each other enough. That my relationship with Richard works so well because it's on a day-to-day basis. I could go on if you like…"

"Are things going well on a day-to-day basis?"

"Yes."

"So what are you afraid would change?"

"Nothing… everything. It doesn't sit well with me that the thought of marrying Richard never crossed my mind until he was down on one knee, proposing."

"If that's what you think, why did you say yes?"

"I told you. He caught me off-guard, I didn't know what to do. I care about Richard and he was there on one knee, offering me all his heart. I said yes, it's what you do when your boyfriend proposes. But now it's giving me anxiety."

"Why don't you talk to Richard about it?"

"And say what? 'Sorry, remember the other night when I said I wanted to marry you? Well… I didn't exactly mean it one hundred percent.' I can't talk to him about it."

"Then you have to decide on your own. But promise me Jake won't feature in it."

"What are you saying?"

"I'm saying you have to decide if you want to marry Richard. I'm saying you should marry him if you love him and want to spend your life with him. And I'm saying the one thing you shouldn't do is not marry Richard because of Jake."

I scowl. "It's not that simple."

"Actually, honey, it is."

Nineteen

A Shared Moment

Saturday, March 3—London

I enter Starbucks sporting a smile so radiant people ought to wear shades.

"I'm engaged," I squeak the moment I reach Amelia. She's sitting at a round table and already has two lattes in front of her.

She gets up with a smile almost as radiant as mine, hugs me for a long time, and settles back down at the table. I join her.

"And you don't seem surprised," I chide her.

"I confess Jake might've asked for some help with the setting up." Amelia smiles mischievously.

"You snitch! You broke the code. You told him about the Jakebox. But I forgive you because it made for the most perfect night of my life."

"Let me see the ring."

I proudly extend my left arm, and the little diamonds on the ring catch the light, sending rainbow sparkles in all directions.

"This is gorgeous."

"It's perfect. Did you help him with this too?"

Amelia shakes her head. "No, he chose it all on his own." She looks at me expectantly. "Tell me everything; I want to know every little detail."

I do tell her everything—well, minus the X-rated parts—and we giggle all along.

"Will you be my maid of honor?" I ask when I'm finished with my report on Jake's proposal.

"Of course I will. Have you already set a date?"

"No, not yet. It's still so new. But sometime within the next year or so. I don't want to do anything big; I'm not a huge fan of big ceremonies."

"Yeah, they're overrated." A bittersweet smile surfaces on her lips. Even if she's moved on, I can see divorcing has left scars on her.

"Definitely overrated," I say supportively. "I want something simple. Just close friends and family."

"U.S. or U.K.?"

"I've no idea! What do you think?"

"You should do it at home. It's where it all started."

"I like the idea… Jake's parents' cabin at the lake would be perfect for a summer wedding. We could set a flowery gazebo just in front of the lake and lay the beach with white chairs…"

"I thought you didn't like wedding planning."

"Well, I don't like planning in general. But the thought of becoming Jake's wife… I want our wedding day to be perfect."

"Whatever you decide, I'm sure it will be."

"But enough about me, what about you and Dylan?"

Her expression becomes bittersweet again. "What about us?"

"Well, how's the living together going?"

"Great, but it's still so new his dirty socks on the bathroom floor haven't started to annoy me yet."

"What is it that males have against laundry baskets?"

"I'm not sure, but they're probably all convinced house elves take care of their discarded underwear."

"Yeah, I bet they do. Dirty socks excluded, how's it going?"

"It's perfect, and I'm even exaggerating on the socks. He's not all that bad. Who am I kidding? Dylan's great. Gem, I'm so happy it scares me. I'm afraid everything will be taken from me when I least expect it."

"I know the feeling. At least you don't have bad karma on your side."

"Meaning?"

"I stole Jake from Sharon, so in theory, bad things should happen to me and good things to her. Whereas in your case, the bad karma should go all to William and the good things all to you. So, really, you're good."

"That's the stupidest thing you've ever said."

I giggle. "Maybe, but I hope your half is true. Do you and Dylan ever talk, uh, marriage?"

"You want to send me running for the hills?"

"Why? Is the idea of marrying Dylan so bad?"

"Gem, I'm not sure I want to get married again; I'm not even divorced yet. And before you say anything," she raises a silencing finger at me, "it's not about Dylan. I don't want to do the whole wedding thing again, like *ever*."

"Is it just the wedding you have a problem with, or is it marriage per se?"

She shrugs. "As I said—this may sound stupid—but I feel last time, getting married ruined everything with William."

"But it wasn't because you got engaged that everything crumbled between you two. You weren't right for each other."

"Mmm, I've been racking my brain, trying to decide when it all started to go wrong. I told you the year before the wedding is a bit of a fuzz. But before that, I've tried to remember when it was that I started loving him less and less and when he drifted away from me… but I can't pinpoint a moment."

"There wouldn't be a specific moment to choose from. Not when it happened so slowly."

"But was it a coincidence that Will began his affair around the time he proposed?"

"No, but it didn't start because he proposed."

"Why then?"

"Okay, I'm not an oracle here, so I don't presume to have a universal knowledge of why Will did what he did. But when he proposed, you guys were probably already having problems…"

"But that's the thing," Amelia interrupts me. "From what I remember, we were doing just fine."

"On the surface maybe, but deep down you probably both sensed something was amiss. And you ignored the thought because it was a scary one. You guys had been together for so long, neither of you could face the idea of leaving the other. So maybe—mmm, subconsciously—getting engaged was a way for you to throw your hearts over the fence. You were drifting apart, and instead of letting go, you found a way to cling to each other even more."

"So your theory is we got engaged out of fear? I remember being happy when Will proposed; I remember *him* being happy."

"As I said, I don't assume I have all the right answers, but think about it—were you *happy*-happy or more… mmm… *relieved*-happy?"

Amelia blinks at me. "Oh. I see what you're saying. When Will proposed, I felt suddenly lighthearted and took it for happiness. But according to you, I was just relieved I didn't have to break up with Will, or even begin to think about breaking up with him, because if he was proposing, surely he was the right man for me. And he probably got the same reassurance when I said, 'Yes.' So if this is what happened, why start an affair a minute later?"

"Ah, this is guesswork again. Maybe it just happened. Maybe he felt reassured on one side, but he started to feel trapped on the other. There's no way to know when he realized he wasn't in love with you, or why he didn't call off the wedding."

"Because he's a coward." Only bitterness shows in Amelia's voice now. "He didn't even have the guts to tell me; he accidentally on purpose left his computer open for me to discover everything and throw him out of the house."

"Yes, he was weak and a coward. He behaved as badly as one could. But Dylan, he's ten times the man William will ever be. And things didn't go wrong because of the engagement or the wedding, they just did. You shouldn't be afraid of being happy; you deserve to be happy more than anyone else does. If you want to marry Dylan, do it."

"It's not like he proposed, we just moved in together."

"Okay, but he might propose one day. And I don't want you to exclude the possibility because of what happened with your ex-husband."

"A marriage that lasted the whole of three weeks, can I even call him an ex-husband?"

"We can call him dung beetle if you prefer."

Amelia cracks her first smile since the wedding talk started. "He is a bit of a dung beetle. And you're right, I shouldn't be scared. I love Dylan, and this time I'm sure it's love with a capital L."

"Giant capital L," I agree.

"If he ever does ask me to be his wife, I'll keep an open mind. Thank you." She hugs me.

"For what?"

"I needed to talk about William and the divorce. And you waited long enough to tell me everything you said today for me to be ready to hear it. You're my best friend in the world; I don't know what I'd do without you."

"You'll never have to find out. Come here." I pull her into another hug, feeling a bit teary.

"Are you crying?" Amelia asks with her chin resting on my shoulder.

"A little bit."

"Me too," she sniffs.

We giggle and cry at the same time. Two friends sharing a moment.

Twenty

Significant Ex

Monday, March 5—London

At the office, I close a document folder, satisfied. My first meeting of the week went well. The negotiation was smooth. Both parties got what they really wanted to begin with. No one relented too much or lost face. As everybody else leaves the room, a lawyer from the other team lingers behind. She's being extra slow in collecting her files from the glass table and she's looking at me with a keen expression I can't interpret.

"Can I help you with something?" I ask.

"I thought you were going to go a lot harder on us. I admire you for not doing it."

Why was she expecting me to hammer her team? Do I have the reputation of a shark?

"We cut a fair deal that made everyone happy, wasn't that the goal?"

"Yes, of course. But sometimes people tend to get personal…"

This conversation isn't making any sense.

"Would there have been a reason for me to get personal with your client?"

"My client, no. Me, on the other hand…"

I stare at her blankly.

"You seriously have no idea who I am."

Why is she giving me a 'you don't know who I am' speech? Who *is* she? I keep staring at her, dumbfounded.

"So you haven't googled me, not even a peek on Facebook. I'm impressed; I certainly didn't have that willpower."

This woman's giving me the creeps. "I'm sorry, but I don't usually google, or stalk on Facebook for that matter, counselors opposing me. If you don't mind, I have another meeting to go to. Have a safe trip back to California."

I turn to leave. I'm almost at the door when she speaks again.

"I'm Jake's wife."

I freeze. My heart starts racing in my chest, pounding blood to my temples. I give myself a couple of seconds to allow my face to go back to presentable as opposed to I'm-about-to-have-a-stroke, and I turn to face my nemesis. Involuntarily my gaze flies over her left hand. There, a delicate rose-gold band is resting on her ring finger. How can such a simple piece of metal cause so much pain? How did I walk into this ambush without knowing anything? I know why! It's all Amelia's fault: she's the one who made me promise never to look this woman up and let me walk into this trap. Unprepared. Unarmed. Strong willpower, my foot. *I would've looked you up the second I had a chance, lady, if it weren't for my I-butt-in-all-situations best friend.*

"You really had no idea," she states.

I shake my head, no. What does she want?

"And to think that I was so nervous about meeting you, I went to a salon to have my hair done. I thought you did the same…"

I furrow my brow questioningly.

"But you didn't. Of course, you'd look like that on a regular day."

I look down at myself and it's nothing that great. I have

my lawyer uniform on—black pencil skirt and white blouse. I stare in horror at the chipped nail polish on one of my fingers, and I ask myself why I chose not to blow-dry my hair this morning. So, I'm sure I'm not that impressive.

I focus on my rival. She's a good-looking woman, with fabulous blonde hair and perfect grooming. Then again, she had the advantage of knowing she'd be standing for this revenge-on-the-ex high noon moment today and went out of her way to look her best. So really, it isn't fair.

"So is there something you wanted to say to me?" I try to smile, but I'm sure I accomplish a grimace at best.

"No, not really. I was just morbidly curious to meet you. I've heard so many stories about you."

Jake talks to her about me? I'm afraid the having-a-stroke face is making a comeback. I swallow a bitter pill as my brain runs free with the knowledge of all the embarrassing things Jake knows about me. How many has he told her? When? Were they discussing it in bed after a passionate night of lovemaking? Am I a running joke between them? Oh gosh, I can feel my teeth grinding.

"I'm sorry, but I can't say I've heard anything about you. So we're not going to be able to swap anecdotes, are we?" I wish my voice wasn't shaking so much. My fake smile has definitely collapsed into grimace territory right now.

"Well, Jake still talks about you a lot…"

"I haven't spoken to Jake in years."

"Well, you're still his significant ex. And I'm sure he's yours…"

If only you knew how much.

"Well, you're his wife. He married you, and I'm engaged." I show her my rock, feeling glad I'm wearing it for the first time since Richard proposed. The thought I nearly had to face Jake's wife unmarried and unengaged is horrific.

"Oh, that's wonderful. When are you getting married?"

"In a year, perhaps two. Anyway, it all worked out for the best in the end." *At least for you*, I add internally.

"Yes. Yes, of course, it did," she says unenthusiastically. She looks at me in a weird way, sad almost. What has she to be sad about? She's married to the love of our lives; she doesn't get to be sad. "I'm sorry if I caught you off-guard. I just wanted to meet you."

"Well, it was very nice meeting you," I lie with a straight face. Lawyer skills and all. "Now if you don't mind I really have to get to that meeting."

"Yeah, sure. Sorry again. I've already stolen too much of your time. Goodbye."

That's not the only thing you stole from me. *"Bye."*

I walk out of the room steadily enough until I'm sure I'm out of sight, then like a drunk person, I brace myself on the walls of the hallway for support. I pinball from left to right until I reach my office, close the door and lock myself in, lowering all the blinds. Finally, I collapse on the couch usually reserved for making clients comfortable—or avoiding them fainting when I give them my invoice, I'm not sure—and cry my heart out.

The pain of losing Jake comes back to me in waves of shock and fear. I'm sobbing so hard I'm hyperventilating. Amelia was right: seeing her face has only made things worse. He did marry lawyer Barbie. Knowing this is the woman Jake goes back to every night, the one he makes love to, the one he has pillow talks with—and about me too, apparently—racks my body with an amount of sorrow I didn't know I had in me. After missing Jake's wedding, I thought I had it bad. But things moved on so quickly with Richard I never really contemplated how Jake was building a family with someone else. I'm nothing more than a distant memory, I've been reduced to the ex he tells amusing stories about.

The thought of that woman knowing things about me stings. It feels like such a violation of my privacy and tells me how little Jake holds dear our relationship—or the memory of our relationship, more accurately. It's a betrayal. He doesn't care anymore; I've become an anecdote to amuse his friends and wife over dinner. What did she say I was? Yeah, his significant ex. She should've said *insignificant ex.* Why does he still have the power to hurt me so badly? Why can't I just stop loving him? Why can't I love Richard the way I love Jake? And what am I doing marrying Richard, anyway? This is too much for one person to bear alone. I need to talk to Amelia.

Twenty-one

Is It Too Late to Say Sorry?

♥♥♥

Monday, March 5—London

I enter the meeting room holding the files of my next settlement case in my arms. I can't help but walk on air around the office surrounded by a halo of happiness. As I move toward my chair, I go over my notes on the terms our client's willing to offer. I glance at the opposing lawyers, who are already seated at the glass table opposite to me, and resume my quick shuffling of documents. That's until my brain registers one of the faces I just glanced at. My halo of happiness shatters as my head jerks back up. I look at the only woman sitting on the other side of the room. Oh gosh, it's *her*! And she's looking at me with a face that says, "Yes, it's me. You wedding-crashing bitch!"

Crap. What do I do now? This is Sharon. The woman I stole Jake from. The woman whose life I ruined. What's she doing in my office? Is she a lawyer? She has to be. Panic floods my body, and as I try to sit, I crash into the chair, sending all my papers flying in the air. This is like one of those forever-embarrassing high school moments. Like walking across the cafeteria, tripping, and splashing the lunch tray on yourself in front of the entire school.

I collect my papers in a dignified way and sit at the grown-ups table, trying to appear respectable. I so wish my face wasn't so hot right now. I must be redder than a chili pepper. And my boss is in the room. Sweat starts pooling under my armpits. At least I'm wearing a white blouse. I hope it doesn't show.

Thank goodness I asked my junior associate to present our proposal today as a learning experience. I wouldn't be able to talk right now. I keep my gaze low and look at my watch under the table. The meeting shouldn't last more than an hour; everything's straightforward and all the parties should be able to get what they're after easily. So no big deal.

"*That is when the opposing counselor doesn't hold the biggest grudge against you,*" says a nasty little voice in my head. All right, Gemma, let's get ready for the longest sixty minutes of your life.

I stay silent for the entire negotiation and only nod here and there at Logan, my junior associate, who's doing a wonderful job with his presentation. I keep my gaze lowered, but I can feel her blue eyes on me most of the time. It's as if she's drilling guilt messages into my skull:

"You stole my husband."

"You ruined my wedding day."

"How does it feel to be this happy at the expense of other people?"

I could die of shame. The way she looked at me. Withering. It was as if I was clubbing a baby seal or something.

"No, you just clubbed her chances at happily ever after. No worries."

I mentally scowl at my sarcastic inner self. I can't believe there's a person in the world who could hate me that much. If ever there was a death stare, Sharon has mastered it.

"Well, when you steal the groom from the glowing bride on her special day, death wishes could easily present themselves as side effects."

"Oh, shut up."

The buzzing noise of people talking in the background suddenly dies away. Did I just say it aloud? I dare to lift my head.

Sharon's staring at me. Apparently, *she* was speaking at that moment.

"I'm sorry, did you say something?" she asks.

I wish the ground would open and swallow me up.

"No, no." If you put together all Ally McBeal's most embarrassing moments they wouldn't add up to this. "Please go on."

"Glad we have your *blessing* to move forward." Sharon gives me a shrewd, evil smile and resumes her speech.

Well, I deserve this. I deserve to be humiliated and shamed. I ruined her life; I took Jake away from her. All her hopes, her dreams of a future with him now are mine. I stole her life. I deserve all the bad shit she wants to give me. What I did to her is bad karma. I need to suck it up and apologize to her. Yes, when the meeting's over I'll own my mistakes and say I'm sorry. Then maybe I won't come back in the next life as a cockroach.

Twenty unbearably long minutes later, the meeting's over. As everyone gets up to leave the room, I linger behind. So does Sharon. It's as if we're both aware we can't just leave without talking to each other. I don't even know if we reached an agreement for our clients, I was too busy rehearsing my apology speech in my head. The last of her remaining colleagues murmurs something in her ear, they exchange a nod, and he's gone. We're alone.

"Err, Sharon. Would you mind having a word with me?" It's the best opening line I can come up with.

"You usually don't ask my permission to talk."

She delivers a jab-cross combo and sends me back to my corner.

"Right, mmm… I really need to talk to you."

"Am I allowed to scream?"

"Please, it's only going to take a minute. You don't know how many times I've thought of picking up the phone to call you."

"Why? Did you leave something out of your last speech?"

She's sharp. Everything she says is a blow to my face. Jab, cross, hook, uppercut, repeat. And since I don't intend to punch back—figuratively speaking—I'm just going to hold my arms in front of my face and parry her verbal assault. She deserves her retribution, and if being mean to me helps her, I'm letting her do it.

"About that. What I did to you was horrible. I never meant for it to happen the way it did. I never meant for it to happen at all. And if there was a way to take it all away, I would…"

"You mean you'd rather not have stolen Jake from me? It seems to have worked out pretty well for you." She jerks her chin at my hand. "Is that from him?"

I follow her gaze to my engagement ring. Oh crap, this is getting worse by the minute.

I blush. "It is. And that's not what I meant. What I wanted to say is that if I could turn back time, I wouldn't wait so long to sort myself out. What I did, the way I did it… it was wrong. But I can't turn back time and I can't take it back. All I can do is to say how sorry I am. I am deeply sorry. I never meant for anyone to get hurt and I know I did hurt you. And I'm sorry for that."

Sharon sighs, shakes her head down, and looks back up at me. "I've never hated someone the way I hated you. That day you took my life in the palm of your hand, crushed it into a ball, and threw it in the trash."

Should I say again how sorry I am? I decide to keep silent and look contrite.

"And you can stop with the beaten-up-dog act."

"It's not an act. I really feel terrible for what I did."

"And what do you expect? What do you want from me? My forgiveness, so you can keep living your life with no remorse?"

"I don't expect anything from you. I owed you an apology, and I wanted to give it to you. That's all. I'm not going to steal any more of your time. Thank you for listening."

I make to exit the room, but she calls me back.

"Wait."

I turn again.

"There's something I want you to hear as well."

"Okay."

"As I said, you're probably the person I hated the most in my entire life. Being left at the altar was the worst experience I ever had. I was lost, heartbroken, humiliated… but," she pauses, "it probably wasn't nearly as bad as going through a divorce would've been, which was probably where Jake and I would've ended up some years down the line. I was in love with him, and being dumped on my wedding day was painful, but not as painful as slowly realizing I'd married someone who could never love me the way I deserve to be loved. I never understood that until I fell for my husband."

I stare at her, stupefied. My eyes travel to her left hand where a tiny gold band is wrapped around her ring finger. Never has a little piece of metal given me more joy than the one sitting on her finger.

"You-you're married?" I stutter.

"Yeah, I eloped to Vegas last month. I couldn't stand to go through the whole ceremony-with-family-and-friends thing again. No crazy-ex-girlfriends-barging-in-to-yell-stop hazards this time."

She's married, and she's making jokes about me ruining her life, which I really didn't do. Right?

"You're married," I repeat, more to convince myself that it's actually true.

"I am, so no matter what happened, I ended up in a good place. As did you, as did Jake, as did my husband. He's your biggest fan!"

"He is?"

"Yeah, he's over there. You can check for yourself."

I stare through the glass wall of the meeting room where a tall, handsome man's smiling at me. He's the counselor who left the room last. His lips part in a warm smile and he bends forward in an obliged bow. I beam at him.

"He came to work for my firm when I was already engaged. He says he fell in love with me during our first joint trial. The day I didn't get married was the happiest day of his life, so you're his hero. Seriously. He was there to pick up the pieces when I broke apart, and a fine job he did. Now I know what real love feels like, and I can understand why you had to do what you did. So all's well that ends well."

I nod as I'm a little too choked up to speak.

"I'd better go now."

"Sure," I say. "And thank you."

She smiles and exits the room. Outside, her husband puts an arm around her waist and pulls her in for a kiss. I watch Sharon literally beam with happiness as the sunrays bounce on her blonde hair, and a huge weight lifts from my chest. My closet's empty; no more skeletons lurking in the dark.

Twenty-two
Doubts

Monday, March 5—London

"At least you've warmed up to the engagement idea," Amelia teases me.

I wave to the barman to bring us another round. We're having drinks in a bar halfway between our offices and I don't care if it is only lunchtime. I'm getting wasted.

"I don't think feeling glad you had a diamond ring to show to your ex's wife qualifies as warming up to the engagement, do you?"

"But you said it was the first time you were happy Richard proposed."

"Just as a social shield. If anything, this is telling me I shouldn't marry Richard even more."

"Why? Because you're in love with a married man you can never have?"

"It's not fair to Richard. I don't love him enough to marry him."

"But you do love him?"

"I do, but it's not consuming, it's not breathtaking. It's just, well, lovely."

"Gemma, what are you going to do if you don't marry Richard? Spend the rest of your life waiting for Jake to suddenly realize he can't live without you? Be single forever? Become a crazy cat lady and die alone?"

"No, no and no."

"What then?"

"I could meet someone else…"

"Someone better than Richard?"

She has a good point there. I'm never going to meet someone better than Richard. He's good-looking, kind, charming, fun, and full of life. His only problem is he's not Jake. I so don't deserve him.

"No, you're right. I'm never going to meet someone better than Richard."

"So?"

"So, I'm screwed." I shake my head. "Richard doesn't deserve this; he deserves a woman who loves him with all her heart and soul. I'd be doing him a favor if I broke up with him now before we're too invested."

"But he loves you, not some hypothetical perfect other woman. You make him happy. You're just freaked out because he proposed."

"But doesn't that say enough about where we stand? Every other woman in my position would be ecstatic—worse even, she would've probably been pressuring her boyfriend to propose. Isn't the fact that the thought never even crossed my mind enough of a telltale?"

"You've never been particularly girly about weddings. When I was telling you the details of my wedding with William, you kept rolling your eyes at everything I said."

"You were a tad overbearing."

"I was a bride," Amelia says with pride. "You'd probably rather elope to Vegas so you don't have to organize anything."

"I would," I admit.

"So, see, you're not your typical girl when it comes to weddings."

"Listen, I'm not scared of the ceremony; I'm scared of

making a life-commitment to a man when I don't really mean it."

"Let's try this way: were you thinking of breaking up with Richard before he proposed?"

"No."

"And since I told you I was moving out, did you think about Richard potentially becoming your new roommate?"

"I might have," I mumble.

"I'm sorry, what was that?"

"Okay, okay. I thought about it. But more like something that would happen in the distant, indefinite future."

"So you were basically planning a long-term future with Richard anyway, except for the married label, right?"

"I've never given it much of a thought, to be honest. I was going with the flow."

"But you still saw yourself with Richard in the future?"

"Near future, yes. I never went past the next couple of months. Isn't that weird? Shouldn't I have been doodling Mrs. Gemma Stratton way before Richard proposed?"

"Let's try out some scenarios. Let's say you were to give Richard his ring back—the thought of never seeing him again wouldn't trouble you in the least?"

"I never said I don't want to see Richard again. I said I'm not sure if I want to marry him."

"Well, darling, you don't have many options left since it's clear he wants to marry you. From where things stand, you can either move forward with Richard or part ways. You can't give him his ring back without breaking up. Is that what you want?"

"No. No! I want things to go back to the way they were last week: easy, uncomplicated. I want to never have met Jake's wife. I want to love Richard the way I still love Jake.

You should've seen the way I cried today. I completely lost it. It's not normal to be that desperate about your ex."

"Listen, Gemma, if I saw the flight attendant in person, I'd cry. Even if it's been ages and I haven't been in love with William for the longest time. It's still a wound. Healed, but the scar's there and it's staying with me for the rest of my life. Please don't throw away a perfectly good man who adores you to chase after the idea of a teenage love. You need to stop trying to replicate what you had with Jake. He was your first love. But it doesn't mean you can't build something even better with Richard. Something real, not a dream."

"Maybe you're right. It's just been a crazy day."

"Imagine if the redhead walked into my office and I didn't know who she was. I'm surprised you didn't pass out when she told you."

"That's the adrenaline for you, prevents you from passing out. It was scary, Ames. She was standing there, telling me how curious she was to meet me after all the stories Jake had told her about me. I wanted to rip her head off."

"I'm sure Jake didn't tell her anything bad. When a person has been so important in your past, it's natural to talk about them."

"I didn't tell Richard stories about Jake."

Amelia raises an eyebrow at me.

"Richard might've asked questions, and I might've answered them," I admit. "But I didn't entertain him with funny anecdotes about my *significant ex*. That's what they call me: the significant ex."

"It could be worse." Amelia smirks.

"You're making fun of my misery."

"I wouldn't dare." She hugs me, still smirking, though.

"Despite the fact that you're such an insensitive best friend, I'm glad you're still living with me, even if it's just for a few more nights. I need you there tonight."

"I'm not going anywhere. Even when I move out, you can count on me whenever you need me."

"You're my rock."

"And you mine."

"Do you think I should tell Richard?"

"That you met Jake's wife?"

"Mmm-hmm."

"If you do, he's going to ask questions, and unless you're ready to answer them, you should keep quiet."

"Questions like what?"

"Like how it made you feel to meet your ex's wife."

"Yeah, you're right. I should keep quiet." I stay silent for a while. "Jake's really gone, isn't he?"

Amelia looks at me with sympathy and nods.

"What am I going to do?"

"Move on and stop looking back."

I give her a confident nod back. But inside my chest, my heart's screaming all its dissent.

***

Want to come over tonight?

When I read Richard's text my heart shrinks.

Sorry, I had a really bad week start

Rain check?

I give amazing feet massages

Perfect to turn around a bad week start

I know, hold that thought for tomorrow

I'm just really tired tonight

I'm also a backstabbing, lying bitch. Because all I want to do tonight is log onto the internet and stalk my ex and his wife, who I met today and who made me cry over how much I hate and envy her. And I don't want to be with Richard because I know the moment he sees my face, he'll be able to tell something's wrong. And I don't want to talk about it, not anymore, especially not with him.

All right babe

I'll leave you to your beauty sleep

Thanks

That feels like another stab at my guilty heart.

Me too

Goodnight

:*

Night

:*

Twenty-three

Save the Date

♥♥♥

Monday, March 5—London

The moment Sharon walks out of the building, I call Amelia and ask her to have lunch with me. We do a complete post-mortem of my meeting with Sharon and she agrees I need to tell Jake immediately. So that night I walk home a bit wary. When I get there, I find Jake already home. He's passed out on the couch and Lucky's nestling on top of his chest. My two boys. I brush the hair off Jake's forehead and kiss him there. Then I scratch Lucky's head. They both look at me from under the lid of one eye.

"Hi." Jake smiles, stretching his arms.

"Hello, sleepyhead. How was your day?" I give him another kiss.

"Exhausting, yours?"

"Mmm, interesting." Why am I so nervous about telling him I met Sharon and that she's married? I have an irrational fear he's going to get jealous or something.

"Interesting, how?"

"I saw Sharon."

"Sharon as in…?" Jake furrows his brows.

"Your ex wife-to-be? Yes." I sit on the couch next to them, level with Jake's chest. "I had a settlement case with a California-based company; she was on the opposing counseling team. I never knew she was a lawyer."

Jake sits up moving Lucky onto his lap and shifts to sit by my side.

"Did you talk?"

"Yes, I finally apologized."

"What did she say?"

"She-she sort of forgave me."

"She did?"

"You seem surprised."

"I am a little. So, was she okay?"

"Yeah, she's married. Eloped to Vegas with a colleague a month ago. She said she didn't want any more crazy-ex-girlfriends hazards."

"Sharon was making jokes about you crashing the wedding?"

"She was. She said not marrying you was the best thing that ever happened to her. No offense."

"None taken."

"She said my little stunt probably saved you two from a painful divorce. She also told me how humiliated and heartbroken she was, and how much she used to hate me. But apparently, I'm her husband's hero for breaking you two apart." I smirk a little. "He'd been secretly in love with her for a long while."

"I think I know the dude."

Is he jealous?

"So how does this make you feel?" I ask.

"Is this a trick question where I can't possibly give a right answer?"

I laugh. "No, no tricks. I swear. I just want to know how you feel about Sharon being married."

"Glad, I suppose."

"No sting?"

"No, definitely not. Sharon's a good person. I'm glad she found her happiness with someone else. I can only wish for them to be as happy as we are."

"That's such a perfect answer you should write a boyfriend manual."

"Hem-hem. Fiancé manual, if I'm not mistaken."

"You most definitely aren't." I kiss him.

He pulls me closer and Lucky protests at being disturbed during his nap.

"Speaking of weddings," Jake says when we finally pull apart, "my mom's pestering me for us to set a date."

"I should keep the mother-in-law happy." I get up to detach a calendar from the kitchen wall. "After all, I owe her a wedding. Did you have any preferences?"

"For the date? No. End of summer?"

I sit back on the couch and leaf through the calendar's pages. "The first of September's a Saturday. It's in six months so we would have enough time to sort everything. How does that sound?"

"First of September. It sounds great!"

"We have a date," I squeal, throwing my arms around his neck, much to Lucky's displeasure. He jumps off the couch, throwing us a resentful evil-kitty glare, and settles himself on the empty armchair in the corner. "Aw, don't be such a sourpuss," I call after him. "We have to celebrate."

"Let me text Mom so she can get off my back."

Jake taps away on his phone and sets it on the coffee table where it starts vibrating at once.

"Does Mrs. Wilder have any other requests?"

"Apparently she wants to know if we've any idea whether we're having the wedding here or at home."

"Okay, this is just an idea, and if you don't like it you can say no. But I was talking to Amelia the other day…"

"Is this where I should get worried?"

"No, don't worry. I'm not going Bridezilla on you. But we were talking, and she suggested we did the wedding at home where it all started, and I immediately knew where I wanted it to be..."

"Well?"

"How'd you feel if we got married at your parents' cabin?"

"I couldn't think of a better place," Jake says in a low voice. His eyes pierce deep into my soul. We're both thinking about our first night together. And in the dark of his irises, I can see the reflection of all my love for him and his for me. It's so intense I'm overwhelmed for a second.

I break the eye contact. "Do you think it'll be a problem for your parents?"

"We can find out."

He taps a reply on his phone, which again vibrates back as soon as Jake drops it on the coffee table.

"What does she say?"

"Here, read for yourself."

I couldn't be happier.

I always knew that girl had some sense in her. Please tell Gemma I can help her as much as she wants with the planning.

With her being there and me being here... but not in a pushy way, of course.

"Be careful here," Jake says. "If you give her an inch of control on the ceremony, she's going to take over completely."

"Can I confess something?"

"Sure."

"I sort of hoped she'd offer to help. I don't care that much for wedding planning. Does that make me a horrible bride-to-be?"

"It makes you the daughter-in-law of the year. She loves throwing parties."

"And she has impeccable taste."

"She does. Do you think *your* mom will get offended if we do it at our house and my mom does all the planning?"

"No. She hates planning parties but adores going to them. And she's going to be thrilled we're going to be at home. Our families are a match made in heaven."

"We're a match made in heaven." Jake lifts my chin with a finger to kiss me.

"You're totally right and impossibly cheesy."

"And you're an insolent little minx who needs a good seeing to."

He manhandles me from the couch, throwing my limp body over one of his broad shoulders, and gets both of us up. I punch him playfully in the back and scream in delight as he drags me toward the bedroom.

Twenty-four

September the First

♦♦♦

Friday, March 9—London

I help Amelia load the last of her boxes into Dylan's car, hug her close, and send her off to her new life. I watch the car disappear around a corner, comforted by the warmth of Richard's body towering behind me.

Back inside my apartment, I take a moment to mentally process all the new empty spots. A vase missing here, a book missing there, nothing big… just all the small telltales of Amelia being gone from the house.

I hug myself. "Feels a bit empty, doesn't it?"

Richard comes up behind me and massages my neck. "Are you sorry Amelia's moved out?"

"Well, yes. Of course. But I'm also happy she's moving in with Dylan. She deserves to be happy after everything that happened to her last year. I'm glad she found him."

"He's a good bloke. And now that you're one roommate short, how'd you feel about taking in another one?"

"No, the roommate I had before Amelia was a nightmare. I'd much rather be alone."

"I promise this roommate won't be a nightmare; he gives the best massages."

I turn to face him. "Oh, you mean you! You want to move in together?"

"We're engaged, so why not?"

"I thought you loved your apartment."

"Yes, I do. I hoped you'd want to move there with me?"

The walls of the apartment seem to close in on us. Call it

cabin fever. "I'd love to," I lie. Too soon, way too soon. "But I just renewed the lease on this place; I've another nine months before it's up."

"Can't you sublet it?"

"No, it's in my contract," I lie again. "But when the lease expires, we can discuss it again."

"I hope a little sooner than that."

"Why?"

"Well, I'd always imagined myself actually living with my wife."

"W-wife? You mean you want to get married right away? Don't engagements last years?"

"They could, but why wait? I want you to become Mrs. Stratton as soon as possible…"

Mrs. Stratton. It sounds so grown up.

"I want to start a family with you, have children…"

"C-children?" I swear the house is shrinking. The walls are imploding.

"And I'm freaking you out big time."

"No, no." I move away from him and go sit on the couch. "It's just that it's all happening so fast. Ten days ago we'd never even discussed getting married and now we're having kids already."

"We're not having kids." Richard smiles at me and sits next to me. "I'm just saying I want them one day after we're married. You want to have children, right?"

"Yes, of course. As you said, one day. It's a huge, scary change."

"It is. So, speaking of weddings, my mum asked me if we'd set a date yet. I told her we'd pick one soon. Want to have a look at the calendar?"

"Sure," I say with the enthusiasm of a zombie.

"Would you prefer a summer or winter wedding?"

"Summer, I guess."

"Me too. What do you say to early September?"

September, next year. Eighteen months from now. A waiting time equal to two consecutive pregnancies should be enough for me to adjust to the idea. "I like September."

"The first is a Saturday; don't you think that'd be perfect?"

"Wait, isn't that this year's calendar?"

"Of course."

"You mean *this* September, as in six months?"

"Yes. Why, don't you?"

Six months from now. Not even one full pregnancy. "Does that leave us enough time to organize everything?"

"That could depend. Do you want a big wedding?"

"No, absolutely not. The simpler, the better."

"Then it shouldn't be a problem to get it running in six months."

I just scored the auto goal of the millennium. "No, I guess not."

"You want to do it here or back in the States?"

"London. Organizing it in the States would be a nightmare." I can't marry Richard in the same town where I met Jake. Definitely not.

"Do you ever miss home?"

"Of course I do."

"Ever thought of moving back?"

"Maybe. Eventually, yeah, it could be a possibility. Would you hate it?"

"Actually, no. I've always had this dream of living in New York, building a business that was mine."

"You want to start a marketing agency? You could do it here."

"I was thinking more an online magazine, a liberal place, a new voice..." He stares up at the ceiling with a dreamy expression. "Would you consider moving to New York?"

"Why New York?"

"It'd be the place to be."

"Is this a real conversation or a hypothetical one?"

"Why, you don't like the Big Apple?"

"Uh. To me, it's just a bigger, dirtier Chicago with less kind people."

We're getting married, having kids, *and* moving to New York? I wonder if Richard is planning to drop any other bombshell on this relationship anytime soon.

"Is everything okay? I'm not really being serious about New York. It's just one of those 'if-you-could-change-your-life-completely-what-would-you-do?' fantasies. You look worried."

I search my brain for something to say to justify my funereal face. "Yes, it's just that… don't take this the wrong way, but I really don't want to plan the wedding. I hate planning events, it stresses me out."

"Don't worry, we'll keep it as basic as it gets."

"You mean you're fine with not having mint-colored birdcages fly open to free a million butterflies as we cut the cake?"

"Is that a thing?"

"If you're Amelia, yeah, it is."

"Don't worry, I don't expect any volatiles. I only want you there."

He kisses me on the forehead and guilt creeps through me.

"I'm calling my parents to tell them."

"Sure, I'll do the same." I use the excuse to take up my phone and walk into my bedroom. I close the door behind me, collapse on the bed, and suppress a frustrated scream by covering my mouth with a pillow.

Six Months Later

Twenty-five

Home

♥♥♥

Saturday, August 25—Chicago Area

Nine days before the wedding, I fly to Chicago with Jake, Amelia, and Dylan. Amelia decided to come with us a week in advance to spend some time with her family and finally introduce Dylan to them. They're staying at an inn in our hometown. As for me, I'm staying at my parents' house in my old room, and Jake's at his parents' too. We're just a block away and it'll be fun to sneak out of the house and rediscover all our old meeting spots in the neighborhood.

We land in Chicago early on Saturday morning and I don't even have the time to take a shower before my mother and sister whisk me away to go shopping for a wedding dress. I know—with just a week to go before the wedding, it's crazy not to have a dress. I'll have to make do with whatever dresses the stores already have in stock, and a week's barely enough time for the fitting. But I'm confident I'll be able to find a wonderful dress in the whole of Chicago, and I want to choose it with both my mom and Kassandra. And given our complicated family geography, I had to do it here.

So here we are. Amelia's coming too—she put Dylan to bed, then joined us at our house in time to leave—as is Mrs. Wilder, Jake's mom. I suspect she put Jake to bed before coming too. And I could use a bit of sleep too after a sleepless night on the long flight from London, but I guess the wedding shopping adrenaline's running strong in my blood because I don't feel as exhausted as I should.

Nonetheless, when the shopping assistant at the wedding store asks me if I'd like a glass of champagne while she shows us some options, I ask her for a double shot espresso instead.

I choose six of the dresses she presents us and leave my audience comfortably settled in plush settees to go change into the first one. The assistant helps me pull it on and pins it at the back to make it fit. When she's done, she gently grabs me by the shoulders and turns me toward the mirror. I blink.

For a second I'm overwhelmed. This is it. I'm getting married. Once the initial shock wears off, I stare at the dress more closely. It's a romantic design made of tulle and Chantilly with a layered skirt. And the bateau neckline is decorated with gemstones. It looks good. But I don't feel any special bonding with it.

I go out to see what the others think.

I've barely walked out and my mom's already in tears. Everyone else seems close to joining her, and even Kassandra's usual swagger is a bit subdued. The shop assistant seems to be the only one aware of my indecision; she squeezes my hand and asks me if I'd like to try some other options. I nod and follow her back to the fitting room.

For the second dress, things go more or less the same: ooohs and aaaahs all around, tears from everyone but me, and a definitive no on my part.

But the moment the shopping assistant pulls up the zipper of the third dress, I know we've found a winner. Finally, tears well up in my eyes, and I take a minute to stare at my reflection before going out to the others. The assistant gives me a knowing nod and leaves me alone in the fitting room to have a private moment with The One Dress.

The gown's in a plain white fabric, with no decorations, beads, or ruffles. It's sleeveless with a bateau neckline and an A-line silhouette. The skirt has some volume and, I discover with delight, side pockets. I swirl to look at the back where a beautiful line of delicate buttons traces my spine. I wipe a few tears from my cheeks and walk out of the room, beaming.

***

After the dress fitting, I'm still not free to go rest as I have to drive to the lake with Mrs. Wilder to oversee the final preparations for next week. Jake's mom has kept me up to date on everything via Skype, but she wants me to approve the last details in person. She still has to give the final okay to the landscape artist for flowers and decorations, to the baker for the wedding cake, and to the guys bringing up the tent she ordered in case it should rain.

Jake's mom walks me around the property with a document holder in her hands, checking away items on her list as I give her my input.

"Flowers, cake, chairs, wedding gazebo, tent, photographer, tables map… we have everything." She looks at me. "Of course, I ordered plastic flats for the ladies in case they don't want to walk on the grass or sand in heels, and shawls should it get cold. We have a delivery of umbrellas coming in, even if the weather forecast's good. Anything else?"

She looks at me then past my shoulder. I follow her gaze and see a team of Ghostbusters approaching, complete with work jumpsuits and proton packs.

"Who are they?"

"Oh dear, I almost forgot. The disinfestation's today,

we'd better go."

"Disinfestation?"

"Yes—we don't want you or the guests fending off mosquitos all night now, do we?"

My chest swells with a wave of gratitude. The last hour has made me appreciate how much pressure Jake's mom took off my plate in organizing this wedding. I launch myself forward and hug her tight.

"Mrs. Wilder, I can't begin to say how grateful I am you did all of this for us."

"Oh hush, dear, it was nothing. And it's about time you started calling me Susan."

"Well, Susan. Thank you so much; I don't know how I'll ever be able to repay you."

"Just make my son happy, and perhaps," she gives me a wicked smile, so similar to Jake's it freaks me out for a second, "grandkids?"

"I'll see what we can do."

"Now let's go before they disinfest us too."

Once I get home, I take a quick shower, ask my mom to wake me up for dinner, and collapse on my bed, finally exhausted.

Twenty-six

Stupid, Stupid Ruffles

♦♦♦

Saturday, August 25—London

A tinge of panic pinches my belly as I stare in the mirror at the millionth wedding gown of the day and feel absolutely nothing. No emotion. No tears. No this-is-The-One-Dress feelings. I'm getting increasingly frustrated with every wrong dress. And positively homicidal toward the shop assistant, who I overheard call me one of the difficult ones.

It's not my fault if she can't find the right dress for me. Okay, I've been a little generic with my requirements, but she's the one who should be able to suggest the right style for me. And the client's always right, so she can wipe that sour expression from her incompetent face.

Or it could be my fault. I shouldn't have left this so late. Finding an already-in-stock dress a week before the wedding is proving more difficult than I anticipated. But I wanted both Kassandra and my mom to be here, and they couldn't come to London too much in advance or take two trips in six months. It's an expensive flight. I should've gone to the States and chosen a dress there.

"Are you ready to go out?" the shop assistant asks.

"No, no point. I don't like this one."

I catch an eye roll in the mirror, but she doesn't say anything. She helps me out of the dress and into the next one. I examine this one in the mirror. It's in a mermaid shape, fitted to the hips with a sweetheart neckline and strapless. The tail part of the skirt's made of ruffled white and blush tulle.

"You want to show the others this one?"

"Sure," I say, unconvinced.

In the main client lounge, I'm met by an unexplainable awed reaction. Everyone seems convinced we have a winner.

"Your face's glowing," my mom says.

"You're so beautiful." Kassandra.

Amelia's speechless.

I try to let their enthusiasm soak under my skin and tentatively smile in the mirror from my pedestal. The shop assistant seizes the momentum and asks me if I want to try a veil. I tell her yes, and she scurries away, happier than I've seen her all day.

She's back in less than a minute and already pinning a short veil with a lace trim on top of my head. She steps back and looks at me expectantly, just like everybody else. I feel so much pressure on me that I don't have the strength to say I don't feel anything for this dress, or any of the other dresses I tried on. So I smile and nod.

My audience erupts in loud whooping and congratulates me. The shop assistant's keeping a neutral face, but it's as if she can read me. Her eyes seem to say, "I know you're faking, but I'm not about to complain. I've earned the commission; you were the client from hell." Okay, maybe her eyes are not that argumentative, but if I were to take a guess, this is what I'd imagine she's thinking.

Back in the fitting room, a seamstress comes to take all my measurements and fit the dress corset and skirt. When everything's pinned in place, the shop assistant helps me out of the gown one last time. She carefully places the dress back on its hanger and finally leaves me alone. I put my clothes on and stare at my wedding dress dangling from its hanger. The ruffles look stupid. I hate ruffles.

"You're hideous," I tell it.

Why did I say I liked this dress? When did I become such

a pushover?

"*Come on, Gemma. You're getting married, the dress isn't important; it's the groom who matters.*" My stomach twists. Okay, let's not go there either. I'm sure every bride's nervous before her wedding, and dresses must be the single most second-guessed item of all weddings.

"Not grooms, though."

Inner self, please shut the hell up.

I put on my I-am-so-happy face again and join the others outside to go to lunch. After we're done eating, I send everyone off doing touristy things around London and go on a maddening wedding suppliers round. I go to Fulham Palace, the wedding venue, to give my final approval to the logistics, flowers compositions, and menu. Then I bring the advance check to the photographer and meet the cake designer to make sure he has the right instructions for delivery. I hate wedding planning.

By the time I get back home, I've barely managed to shower before we go out again. Richard and I take my family to a restaurant. Unfortunately, even dinner turns out to be too much of a formal affair. Everyone is making an effort, but the conversation's stiff at best. That's when I realize my parents don't know my future husband, like, *at all*. Richard's being as charming as ever, but they lack that mutual coziness, which can only come from years of mutual interactions.

"Like it was with Jake."

Ah, Gemma, don't go there. I swat the thought away like an annoying fly.

I find it hard to enjoy the fine dining when the atmosphere's so awkward. The only person not having difficulties is Kassandra. She's stuffing her mouth full of as much food as she can take, very much resembling a chipmunk. She doesn't have a problem making conversation either, talking to Richard as if she'd known him her entire life. Then again, she does that with everyone.

To be fair, Richard's parents don't know me any better. They live up north, and we've only been to visit them a couple of times. These things take time, and we have the rest of our lives for our families to get cozy with each other.

A server finally brings the check and Richard and my dad squabble over who should take it. Dad wins in the end. So Richard insists on paying for the taxi ride home. My parents are staying in my spare bedroom and my sister's sleeping in mine. I usually stay at Richard's house, but Kassandra insisted on me staying here with them tonight.

"Are you coming back with me?" Richard asks after saying goodnight to everyone else.

"No, not tonight. Kassandra asked me to stay."

Richard purses his lips.

"You know something?" He leans in to give me a goodnight kiss. "It's your hen party tomorrow," he whispers in my ear, "but I didn't say anything." He winks at me and hops back into the cab to go home.

***

"Shouldn't you be further ahead with the packing?" Kassandra asks once we're both tucked into my queen bed.

"Nah, my lease doesn't expire for another three months. I've all the time in the world to pack."

"Okay, but shouldn't you at least have started? Aren't you moving in with Richard next week?"

"Why are you so concerned about my packing?"

"I'm not. You're a bit touchy, you know?"

"Sorry. It's all this wedding planning… I hate it. It's like having a second job on top of mine. Why couldn't I get one of those butt-in mothers-in-law who wanted to organize everything?"

"You mean Richard's mom refused to help?"

"No, no. Not at all. I never asked, and she never offered. She doesn't even live in London, so there's not much she could've done, anyway. I just wish I had a party planning mother-in-law, that's all."

Kassandra throws me a piercing stare and I know we're both thinking what we're not saying: "Like Jake's mom."

"We should sleep now," my sister says.

"Why?" I pretend not to know anything.

"Because we have an early start tomorrow."

"Why?"

She beams at me. "It's your bachelorette party. We have a full schedule so you'd better get your beauty sleep."

"What have you planned?"

Kassandra closes a phantom zipper over her mouth. "My lips are shut."

"Oh, come on. Tell me."

"Nope."

I tickle her sides. "Tell me, tell me, tell me."

She squeals like a pig but doesn't spill the beans. As the screeches increase in volume, my dad pounds a fist on the wall, yelling, "Be quiet, girls."

"Yes, Daddy," we chorus.

Just like old times.

Kassandra turns off the light and we fall asleep, holding hands like we used to do as kids when my baby sister sneaked into my room because she was afraid of the dark. Only tonight, I'm the one who's afraid. Of the dark, of where my life's going. I'm scared I'm about to make the biggest mistake of my life.

Kassandra gives my hand a gentle squeeze and I relax a bit. Everything's going to be okay. It has to be.

Twenty-seven

Remember That Time?

Saturday, August 25—Chicago Area

After dinner, I'm unpacking in my bedroom when a familiar *tap-tap-tap* noise drives me to the window. I open it and lean forward on the bottom rail. Jake's standing in the shadows of my backyard, throwing pebbles at my window as he used to when we were teenagers and he wanted me to come out after-hours. Unnecessary, but utterly romantic. For a second I'm tempted to use my childhood escape route and climb out the window and down the flower trellis, but I don't want to break a leg—good luck notwithstanding—a week before the wedding. Instead, I blow Jake a kiss and ask him to wait for me on the front porch. He gives me a military salute and walks around the house.

Downstairs, I find my parents watching the news in the living room.

"I'm going out for a walk with Jake," I tell them.

"Not too keen on climbing out the window anymore?" my dad asks with a smirk.

I stop dead in my tracks. "You knew about that?"

"And many other things. You'd be surprised, sweetie pie."

"I don't want to know," I say truthfully.

"Have fun, pie."

I wave goodbye and join Jake on the porch. He wraps his arms around my waist and pulls me down to the grass while I kiss him.

"To the river?" he whispers in my neck.

"To the river."

As if no time has passed at all, we stroll toward our favorite secret spot. Even if now I'm not so sure whether it was that big a secret.

"You know how all these years we thought we were being so smart?" I ask.

"Mmm-hmm."

"Well, it appears we were so busted instead."

I tell Jake about my dad. He laughs heartedly.

"Do you think it's the same with your parents?"

"Maybe—probably."

I blush. "I hope at least they don't know about the lake cabin. That'd be so embarrassing."

We reach our favorite bend in the river and Jake spreads a blanket on the grass in a spot where we're sheltered from the road by the trees but can gaze up at the stars. We lie down next to each other and stare up at the night sky.

"Remember the first time we came here?" Jake asks, rolling over to face me.

"You mean the night you didn't kiss me for the first time? Hard to forget—I cried about it for a week. I thought you didn't like me enough to kiss me."

"I liked you too much to kiss you." He kisses the tip of my nose and electric currents shoot from where his lips touched my skin to my cheeks, making them burn red. After all these years, he can still make me blush. "I'd never kissed anyone, and I was scared you'd think I was a bad kisser."

"I hadn't kissed anyone either, so I wouldn't have been able to tell."

"Well, I didn't know that at the time. It took me a while to work out the courage to finally kiss you."

"Jake Wilder," I pull him closer by the neck of his shirt, "I'm so glad you did."

We kiss for a long time until Jake pulls back. "Did you find the dress?"

"Yes." I beam. "And it's wonderful, it's…"

He places a finger on my lips. "Shhh. Don't tell me anything, I want it to be a surprise."

"Of course I'm not telling you anything. What about you? Did you sleep all day?"

"Not all day." He pinches my nose affectionately. "When you and my mom came back, she made me drive her around town all afternoon. I didn't know a wedding required so much work."

"Oh Jake, your mom has been awesome. We couldn't have done it without her. We should do something for her."

"She just wants grandkids."

"And what do you say about that?"

"That I can't wait to start working on it." He bites my earlobe, knowing it makes me lose my mind.

I push him back. "Mr. Wilder, I'm sorry, but we're old-fashioned here. You're not getting lucky until the honeymoon. Can you believe we're finally going to Hawaii?"

"I can't wait to be on a white sand beach with you. But for old times' sake, we should take a trip to the cabin." He bites me again. "To oversee the final details, obviously."

"We're not going near that cabin before our wedding day." I stifle a yawn. "Besides, the place's under disinfestation."

"You're falling asleep on me." He gets up and offers me his hands to pull me up. "I'm taking you home."

We walk back to the street. "Tomorrow I want to sleep all

day," I say.

"I'm afraid that's not going to happen."

"Why?"

"Our friends have organized our bachelor and bachelorette parties tomorrow."

"Oh, where are they taking you?"

"No idea."

"Where are they taking me?"

"I know nothing."

We stop outside my house. "Promise me you won't wake up on a hotel roof in Vegas, not remembering anything that happened to you."

Jake laughs. "That's an easy promise to make. Honestly, it's just going to be a fishing trip with beers and burgers afterward."

"Aw, you think the girls will get me burgers too?" I lift my arms in front of my face, holding an invisible burger in my hands. "I want real, fat American burgers."

"I'm positive they'll have some burgers for you at some point."

"This is good night then." I'm leaning in to kiss him when the porch lights flash on.

"Did your dad just turn on the lights on purpose?"

"Old habits die hard, I guess." I give Jake a quick peck on the lips and run inside the house.

Twenty-eight

Champagne Tea and Tarot Cards

♦♦♦

Sunday, August 26—London

I wake up with screaming in my ears. My sister yells, "Wakey, wakey. It's bachelorette party time."

I smother her with a pillow. "Go away, I want to sleep."

"Come on." She throws the blankets away from my body. "You can sleep later. The first part of the day's at a spa."

That does it for me. The only thing I can use more than sleep right now is a relaxing massage.

"You can dress casual for now; we have your other outfits planned for you."

"Yes, sir."

I abide by the dress code and join everyone else in the kitchen for breakfast. My nostrils flare with the aroma of cinnamon and sugar. Mom's cooking and Amelia's laying the table. Exactly like she used to do when she came over to my house for breakfast back in the States.

Mom hands me a plate filled with her best recipe cinnamon French toast. "My sole contribution to your bachelorette party is to make you your favorite breakfast."

"Thank you, Mom. What are you and Dad doing today?"

"Don't worry, we're sightseeing. You go have fun," she tells me, then scowls at Kassandra. "Not too much fun."

Kassandra mumbles something unintelligible as her mouth's too full of bread for her to speak.

"Who else is coming?" I ask Amelia.

"Your friends from work. And Mary and Jessica were the

only ones able to make it from back home. They're going to take a trip to Paris on the Eurostar next week and come back in time for the wedding. All the others said they could make it only to the wedding."

"Wait—you didn't invite Flotsam and Jetsam?"

"I can call them if you like."

"Absolutely not." We laugh. "I'm ready for my pampering. Let's go."

We move through London in a rented black limo equipped with champagne and all sorts of spirits. The others meet us at the spa. We stay there until four in the afternoon, getting every beauty treatment ever heard of. After the spa, we go to the Waldorf for their champagne afternoon tea. Amelia and Kassie decided an afternoon tea somewhere for a British hen party was fun, and I completely agree. From the Waldorf, we move on to a boutique perfume shop where we all make customized scents.

I enter the limo, holding my little perfume bottle. "I'm hungry," I say.

"We've another stop before dinner," Amelia says.

"But I'm starving," I protest. "Where are we going for dinner?"

"It's gourmet burgers for you, but only if you're good and behave."

"You can drink champagne if you're hungry," Kassandra says, passing me a flute of bubbly.

I'm not sure it's a good idea on an empty stomach, but I take it all the same.

Two glasses of bubbly later, the limo stops in front of a nondescript building in an area of London I'm not familiar with.

"Where are we?" I ask.

“We’re at the Psychic Sisters.”

“To do what exactly?”

“We’re going to have our fortunes told.”

A round of excited giggles spreads around the back of the limo.

“Oh, you know it’s nonsense,” I whisper in Amelia’s ear.

“It might be nonsense, but it’s fun. Come on, everyone said this was an absolute bachelorette party must.”

Amelia takes my hand and drags me out of the car and inside the building. We enter a sort of office worthy of Whoopi Goldberg’s house in *Ghost*. The hall opens on to three different rooms, apparently each reserved for a gifted diviner sister. We split into three groups and queue in front of the different doors. Amelia and I are at the front of the middle one and we’re ushered in at once.

Inside, the atmosphere’s kind of dark and gloomy. The air is suffocating and impregnated with the smells of cedar wood and jasmine coming from some incenses burning in a corner.

“Welcome, dears.” An old crone with black hair and yellowish eyes greets us from the farthest corner. She’s so small crouching behind a wooden desk, I hadn’t noticed her when we got in. “Come, come, have your future unraveled.”

We take our seats in two ancient looking armchairs. I take in the chandelier dangling from the ceiling, the baroque style of my armchair, and the ridiculous costume the hag’s wearing, and I’m tempted to snort. I hope we’re not spending too much on this old fraud.

“You have a specific question you’d like to ask the cards?” the crone asks us, unfazed. Apparently, she isn’t getting my incredulity vibes. “You want to know about your past lives, parallel lives, or about your present life?”

“Make it about her love life,” Amelia answers for me.

"The True Love spread then, very well. Take the cards, dear, mix them, and cut the deck for me, please."

I do as instructed and then pass the deck to the crone who spreads it in a semicircle of sparkling blue and gold cards.

"Now pick six cards and pass them to me one by one. Let the energy in your hands guide you to the right cards."

I pick the cards at random, not feeling any particular chakra energy flowing from my fingertips, and hand them to the crone.

The fortuneteller puts the first and second card in a row at the top, the next three cards in a row below, and the last one at the bottom, alone. She turns the first two cards.

"The Fool reversed for you—it seems you're a bit of a reckless soul. And for your other half, The Tower. Interesting." She gives a little smile.

"I-interesting how exactly?" I stutter.

"The Tower symbolizes upheaval and a sudden change."

"You mean because we're getting married?"

"Perhaps, or perhaps not. Let's see what the other cards have to say." She smiles knowingly.

So far, so *bad.* The other three cards are unveiled next.

"The Wheel of Fortune for the thread that connects you to your love. The Wheel of Fortune's a powerful card. It represents karma—you can't escape it. Next, The Devil, reversed, for your strengths. It states you're ready to take control. As for your weaknesses, Judgment. This one tells you to pay heed to your inner calling."

"Meaning?"

"In simpler words, follow your guts. Trust your instinct."

Whatever. "Great advice," I say awkwardly.

"And now the final card, the True Love card. The one that reveals if your relationship can be successful." She turns it and stares at it silently for a while before fixating her yellow eyes on me. "Death."

"Oh, that sounds promising." I snort.

"Death, my dear, is a symbol of transformation and of new beginnings."

"So what do you make of this entire… uh," I try to remember the word she used, "spread?"

"You're about to meet your fate."

"So, I'm—uh—not making a mistake getting married?"

"When the moment comes, just follow your heart, darling, and you'll be fine."

I don't pay much attention as Amelia gets her future predicted, and when we leave the room, it isn't one minute too soon for me. The old hag has unsettled me.

We wait for the others in the limo, and I hope those burgers really are gourmet because I need a cheer up after that ominous Death card.

The burgers *are* great. After two or three cocktails, any thought of a relationship's demise flies out of my head and I'm cozily beginning to feel ready for bed. Amelia seems to have read my mind when she announces the final stop of my party.

"And now, ladies, back to my house for a pajama party and a showing of all our favorite Molly Ringwald movies."

I cheer along with the others. "Thank you for making this day so special," I whisper to Amelia.

She hushes me.

"Where did you put Dylan? Is he watching Molly Ringwald with us?"

"He's staying at Richard's. They're having his stag party tonight too."

"Oh gosh, I hope they don't buy him strippers."

"I specifically forbade it."

I squeeze her arm to thank her as we walk toward the limo, holding each other. That's until Kassandra barrels into us from behind, wriggling herself in between us and wrapping one arm around our shoulders.

"I'm so glad we have the limo to go home." She slurs her words a bit. "I could never figure how to drive on the wrong side of the road."

I smile, nod, and silently add that driving on the right side of the road wouldn't make much of a difference for her tonight.

Twenty-nine
Bridesmaid Wars

Sunday, August 26—Chicago Area

"You know, orange really *isn't* the new black." I eye Amelia sideways as she enters my old bedroom at my parents' house. "Why are you wearing a puffy orange meringue?"

She beams at me. "It's bachelorette party day! Almost a week before the wedding, so you'll have time to recoup."

"Recoup from what?"

"It's a surprise. Here's your outfit." She hands me a bridesmaid gown I had to wear at a cousin's wedding many years ago and that I honestly thought I'd burned. I gingerly take the dress from her.

"Are we trying to get arrested by the Fashion Police?" The thing is a cotton candy nightmare of ruffles, sheer fabric, and bows. "Do I really have to wear this?"

"Yes, it's going to be fun. Trust me!"

"I don't see how it's going to be fun unless we're doing a fashion exorcism."

"Stop complaining and get dressed!"

Kassandra bursts into the room clad in a heinous maroon tablecloth. "Is she whining about the dress?"

"Yes, she is."

"It's lucky I managed to find the headpiece then." She regards me with an evil grin, shaking the flowery tiara in her hands. "Chop, chop, sistah. We don't have all day."

I reluctantly pull on the dress, which strangely enough still fits, while Amelia secures the tiara on my head with some bobby pins. When she's done, she pulls my zipper up and I'm ready to go wherever they're taking me.

"Ta-dah! I'm the bridesmaid from hell. You two happy?"

"Very." Kassandra nods with approval. "You're missing the shoes." She hands me a pair of white sneakers.

I look at their feet for the first time and see they're both wearing sneakers as well. What the hell have they planned for the bachelorette party? I put on a pair of socks and lace up the shoes as further complaints would be useless.

"Everybody else is already here," Kassandra frets. "Let's go before we're late."

We shout our goodbyes to my parents and stream onto the front porch where I halt, shocked. Parked in front of my house is a white limo, and lined up in front of it are all my closest friends from high school, college, and even a couple who made the trip from London. They're all dressed in heinous bridesmaid gowns and sneakers—they make the final lineup from *27 Dresses* look like a classy display in comparison. It's a vengeance of ruffles, of flowered curtain-style prints, of pajama dresses, foil fabrics, and frilly frocks. It looks so horrible I'm starting to believe it's brilliant.

I jump the few steps down the porch and run across the garden to greet everyone. It takes a few minutes before Kassandra herds us into the car where I keep going with the catching up—with the added perk of champagne and the soundtrack from *Sixteen Candles* playing in the background. The eighties songs actually go really well with our dresses.

The journey to our destination takes about half an hour, and when the car stops my friends and I swoop out in a rush of colored tulle. We're standing on dry grass in front of a massive barn. The building's standing on the side of what looks like a larger roving amusement park. When we exit the limo, the driver leaves to go park somewhere, and I spot a guy dressed in military gear and boots heading our way.

"Ladies, welcome," he greets us with a slight Southern lilt. "Please follow me."

He beckons us into the barn. Inside, we form an orderly line. We're surrounded by racks of military green rifles—plastic I assume, or hope at least—white working jumpsuits, and plastic goggles.

"Good morning, ladies, and welcome to Paintball Wars Game Center. Rules are simple," military guy tells us without preambles. "On the field, you must wear your goggles at all times, no exception."

He hands us each a plastic mask.

"Paintball Wars?" I mouth to Amelia.

This is brilliant, and finally, the dresses make sense. We're going to take revenge on the bridesmaid dresses from hell and splatter them in paint.

"These are your weapons," military guy continues. "You unlock them like this." He shows us how to remove the barrel plug. "You aim and pull the trigger to shoot. No blind shooting's allowed at any time. You have a bag of ammo each. You load them here." He shows us where to insert the paint balls. "If you're hit, you're dead. Plug your barrel and move off the field. All right, that's all, ladies. Go have fun."

The game starts, and it's hilarious. Right from the beginning, it's obvious most of us—myself included—have never played paintball before, but we're all good sports and it makes for the most comical hour and a half of my life. Watching my friends trip on their floor-length satin dresses as they try to pull off sneak attacks, or seeing them dive behind a barricade, dress trains flowing in the air as they go down, is priceless. Amelia also hired a photographer to document the battle. We take silly shot after silly shot in our frilly dresses and plastic rifles.

When the game's over—I'm not even sure who won or if I'm still "alive"—my friends lead me to the other side of the barn where I'm hit by a cloud of grill smoke. A table laid with pretty colored cocktails and a hamburger extravaganza awaits us. My mouth waters at the sight—after an hour of running this is like a dream come true. We sit at the table, all of us still wearing our bridesmaid dresses—some looking more worse for wear than others after the paint riddle—and sporting thirty-two-teeth smiles.

After stuffing my mouth with as many burgers as my body can handle—I know, bad for my bride-to-be diet—we stroll through the rest of the amusement park, playing different games and going on the various rides. It's fun to see the disbelieving looks our colorful attire wins us. We're shuffling around the various stands—I'm contemplating getting real cotton candy to match my dress—when Amelia stops in front of a blue and yellow pointy tent with a red silk door.

"You should get your fortune read," Amelia suggests.

"Oh, no. It's just a bunch of crap."

"Crap or not, it's fun. Come on, I'll do it with you."

We go inside, and it's as if we've entered a different world. The noise from the circus outside is dimmed in here, and the atmosphere's dark. The tent smells like cedar wood and jasmine, and the mixed scent seems inexplicably familiar. There are incense sticks burning in a corner. That must be it: I must have been in some other place with the same incenses at some point if my life, even if I can't remember where. Gosh, the air's suffocating.

"Welcome, dears," an old crone greets us from the

farthest corner. As I look at her and take in her black hair and yellow eyes, a powerful sense of déjà vu attacks me. "Oh, it's you," the crone says. "I've been waiting for you for a while now."

"You have?"

"Oh, yes. I wondered how you'd turn up in this life."

It's probably all an act to set the divination atmosphere right, but she gives me goosebumps all the same.

"Maybe this wasn't a good idea," I whisper to Amelia.

"Come on, don't be a chicken!" She grabs my hand and drags me forward in front of the diviner. Amelia and I each pick one of two short stools waiting empty in front of the tiny card table.

"My friend would like to have her fortune told," Amelia says.

"I know, dear," the hag says. "The True Love spread then, right? Do you remember what to do?"

"Err… no?"

"Pity. Take the cards, mix them, and cut the deck for me, please."

I gingerly do as I'm told. Once the crone has her deck back, she spreads it in a semicircle of sparkling blue and gold cards.

"Pick six cards from me and pass them to me one by one. Remember, let your interior energy guide your fingers."

I pick the cards randomly, not feeling any particular force guiding me as I do, and hand them to her.

The fortuneteller puts the first and second card in a row at the top, three cards in a row below, and one at the bottom, alone. She turns the first two cards.

"The Star for you and The Magician for your other half. He's a powerful, resourceful man and you're a pool of serenity and confidence surrounding your love. Much better this time around, aren't we?"

What does she mean this time around? As if I were having my fortune told every other day. But so far, so good, so I nod and smile.

She turns the second row of cards.

"The Wheel of Fortune for the connection between you—we already knew that. You have a powerful destiny awaiting you. The High Priestess for your strengths. Interesting how things change." She gives a little smile.

"C-change?" I stutter.

"Yes, dear. Change. The Priestess is a symbol of steadiness and calm."

"Good, I guess."

"Good indeed. As for your weaknesses," she looks at the last card of the row. "But of course, The Emperor, reversed."

"What does the Emperor mean?"

"Upright, it is a symbol of structure. Reversed, it shows a desire for domination, excessive control, rigidity, and inflexibility. Which was what got you into trouble in the first place, wasn't it?"

I swallow at the accuracy of her statement. It was pride and my unchecked need to feel in control that ruined things with Jake last time. I'm never letting my pride or the necessity to affirm myself through my job get in the way of my relationship ever again.

Amelia smirks beside me, and I kick her sideways in the shins.

"And now the final card, the True Love card. The one that reveals if your relationship can be successful." She turns it and stares at it silently for a while before fixating her yellow eyes on me. "The Lovers."

I blink at her.

"Well, it doesn't get any better than this now, does it?"

"I-I suppose?"

"Oh, darling, of course, you do."

"So what do you make of this entire... uh," I try to remember the word she used, "spread?"

"You're right where you should be, nothing to worry about." She winks.

I don't know what to make of this assessment. It seems just like a ball of nonsense to me.

Once Amelia has had her future predicted as well, we exit the tent and rally the others for the final stop of my party.

"Where are we headed next?" I ask my sister as she tackles me from behind. She's definitely had many more drinks since lunch.

"Oh, you're going to love this! We rented the old drive-in, and they're doing a special showing of *Sixteen Candles* just for us!"

I squeak and giggle with joy while jumping and clapping my hands. "Thank you, both of you..." I brace one arm over Amelia's shoulders and one over Kassandra's. "This has been the best day of my life."

"Eeeeee." My sister winks at me. "Wait until you see Jake in a tux waiting for you at the altar before giving away the best day prize."

I giggle again and we head toward the limo where the driver's patiently waiting for us in the parking lot. Watching my favorite movie in an old drive-in is the perfect ending to a perfect day.

"Wait, how are we going to watch the movie from the limo?"

"They're giving us the Cadillacs in the front row,"

Amelia says. “Real fifties style.”

“The limo’s just for driving us home after the movie,” Kassandra explains.

I smile and silently add that she’ll probably need a lift home more than anyone else will.

Thirty
Cold Feet

♦♦♦

Saturday, September 1—London

On my wedding day, I wake up at the crack of dawn with the alarm clock drilling a hole into my skull. It takes a long while for everything to get started. Even if I have planned every last detail, somehow it still seems I have a great deal left to do. Mom's so nervous she burns breakfast and I spend a good ten minutes telling her it's okay and send Dad to grab some muffins from the next-door bakery. Kassandra appears in the living room already dressed in her bridesmaid gown and I send her back to my room to change. I don't want a coffee-stained bridesmaid.

The makeup artist is late, and she squabbles with the hair stylist. But they manage to get Kassandra, Amelia—who arrived at my house at some point during the morning—my mom, and I ready in time. At noon, we eat cold sandwiches, and half an hour later, a car's here to pick us up. I clamber in the back with my mom and Kassandra, and Amelia hands us my wedding gown that we lay across our laps to minimize wrinkles. Dylan should come to pick up Amelia shortly and bring along the hair stylist and makeup artist for on-site retouches. My dad climbs in the front seat and, at last, we're ready to go. The driver starts the engine and the car flings forward into London's traffic. I barely have time to wonder how long the journey will take when we're back. Kassandra forgot her clutch. We're not exactly late, but I'm getting anxious. Luckily, we reach Fulham Palace with time to spare before the ceremony, and all I have left to do is slip into my white dress and wait for the guests to arrive.

My mom pulls up the zipper of my wedding gown and flashes me a proud smile in the mirror. Her eyes glistening with unshed tears, she makes me emotional too.

"You look perfect." She squeezes my shoulders gently. "I'm going to give you a minute."

"Thanks, Mom." I squeeze her hand in return before she exits the dressing room I've been given to get changed in.

I stare at my reflection in the mirror, trying to decide how I feel. I feel like the last six months have rolled me over. Since Richard proposed, it's as if my life's slipped out of my hands. Decisions have been made, venues, dresses, meal courses have been chosen, and I let it all flow past me. As if it wasn't my life that was being decided; as if it wasn't my wedding. But I can't escape the fact that this *is* my wedding day. That today I'm pledging to love one man, and one man only, for the rest of my life. Looking at myself in my white dress, I think of a man other than my fiancé.

I moved across the world to forget him. I burned all memories of him. I've refused to even voice his name for months now. But he always finds his way back into my heart. Is this how Jake felt on his wedding day? As if he was saying his final goodbye to me at that moment? I doubt he spared me a thought.

Amelia bursts into the dressing room and stops as she spots me. "You look… oh gosh, I don't have the words. I'm going to cry."

"That makes two of us," I sob.

"Gemma, what's going on?" Amelia shuts the door behind her before rushing to my side. "Are you overwhelmed by emotions? Nerves?"

"No, I'm just being stupid. I couldn't help thinking about him just now. How this is goodbye, for good."

"*Him*? Are you… you mean Jake?" Amelia asks in a shaking voice.

I nod.

Amelia looks at me aghast. "But you haven't spoken about him in forever, not since…" She searches in her memory for the last time his name came up. "Not since you met Sharon, ages ago."

"Well, you chided me every time I tried to talk about him. But you were right: he's married and I've no business thinking about him on my wedding day."

Amelia grimaces and blushes tomato red.

"What?"

"Nothing."

"Ames, don't say, 'Nothing.' You couldn't look any less *nothing*."

"Okay, but promise me you won't freak out… this is the worst time, really… I probably shouldn't…"

"Freak out about what? What is it? You're making me freak out by not telling me whatever the hell it is you're not telling me."

"Why don't we sit down?"

"I can't. Whenever I try to sit I'm stabbed by the boning—. I hate this dress; I don't know why I bought it, and if you don't start speaking soon, I'm going to scream."

"Okay, okay. But *I'm* sitting down." She also takes a flute of champagne and downs it in one sip. "Now, try not to get mad. But I thought it was better not to tell you…"

I narrow my eyes at her. "Not to tell me *what*?"

"You seemed finally happy, so I didn't want to stir up useless doubts. You'd finally stopped talking about Jake, and I had no idea you'd just stopped *talking* about him, but not thinking about him…"

"So what? If you're about to give me a lecture, I'm not in

the mood."

"No, no lecture. Gem, I'm so sorry I didn't tell you…"

I watch her wring her fingers in agony. "Out with it," I hiss.

"It was some time ago, I bumped into Jake…"

"You what? I don't understand. When did you go to San Francisco?"

She shakes her head. "I didn't. It was here in London."

"What was Jake doing in London?"

"He-he sort of m-moved here."

"I need to sit down."

"But the boning."

"I'll take the stabbing, and a glass of that too." I point at the champagne and Amelia pours me a glass. "So he's moved here with *her*?"

London's *my* city.

"Without," Amelia whispers.

"So she lives in San Francisco and Jake lives in London. I'm not following you."

"Oh, Gem. Jake got… Jake got d-divorced!"

I shoot out of the chair as if I've been given an electric shock. Actually, my body did give me an electric shock, like when you're sleeping and your body thinks you're dying so it electrocutes you. I pace in circles around the room.

"Tell me everything you said to him and everything he said back."

"Gemma, this isn't a good idea."

"Not telling me Jake got divorced was the bad idea. How could you?"

"I'm sorry, but you seemed finally happy."

"Do I look happy now?"

"Not so much."

"I need you to tell me everything. When did he get

divorced?"

"He told me they started discussing a separation in early April this year,"

"But that's just after I met his wife in my office. When was it? Right after Richard proposed, so first days of March. That explains the melancholy expression she had. Did he say why they got divorced?" My brain and my heart are in a race to decide which one's frying faster. And adrenaline's fueling them both.

"Something about understanding they weren't right for each other."

"So when did he move here?"

"Two months ago, early July."

Jake. Wifeless. Living in my city for two months. And I didn't know. What if I passed him on the street and did not see him?

"Did he say why London?" I'm not letting myself hope yet.

"He said The London Clinic offered him a research position here a year ago, around the time he got married. He refused it at the time, but they kept insisting… offering him bigger and bigger salaries and more and more research independence every time. So when they renewed the offer just after he'd signed the divorce papers, he finally took it."

Uh, not what I expected. What did I expect?

"Did he… hem… ask about me?"

"Yes, he asked how you were and told me he knew you were engaged and asked when the wedding was."

"I told Sharon that day in my office and she must've told him. What next?"

"I told him you were getting married the first of September at Fulham Palace, so he told me to give you his felicitations."

My heart seems to be winning the race for the more stressed organ. "Did he… did he say anything else?"

"No, he told me to take care and went on his way."

I collapse back on the chair and my sides pay for it as I receive a vicious stab from the corset.

"How did he look when he asked about my wedding? Sad? Genuinely happy? Indifferent?"

"He didn't have any particular look. Listen, Gemma, it was a five-minute conversation on the street, nothing more."

"Nothing more? How can you say that? Jake living here, in my city, single! And you say, 'Nothing more.' How could you not tell me? I could've… I could've…"

"What? Canceled the wedding?"

I don't need to tell her that's exactly what I'd been thinking because she knows.

"This is exactly why I didn't tell you," she says fiercely.

"You don't get to decide how I should live my life. You should've told me."

"And what? Watch you throw away a wonderful man who simply adores you to chase after a memory?"

"Don't you think it's destiny Jake ending up here, of all places? And after all this time, just when he got divorced. He married the wrong person. You almost married the wrong person. Maybe I'm about to marry the wrong person too."

"So tell me. In the two months Jake's been here, how many times did he call you?"

"He doesn't have my number."

"You've been working at the same firm since you moved here. If he wanted to contact you, all he had to do was call your office."

"Maybe he thinks I don't want him to call me. I left him. I never answered any of his calls. I never told him I still loved him… and if I did…"

"What? You'd get back together with him? Do you even know Jake? When was the last time you spoke to him?"

I blink at her, get up again, and move toward the door, giving Amelia my shoulders. *I need to think.*

"Listen, I'm not saying you should marry Richard at all costs," Amelia says. "Tell me you don't love Richard and you don't have to say another word. I'll get you out of here and take care of everything. The guests, the minister, your parents…"

At that instant, the door bursts open again and I see a brief image of Richard looking dashing and full of life in his tuxedo before he closes the door again.

"Sorry, wrong room!" he shouts from the other side. "I know it's bad luck to see the bride before the ceremony, but I'm glad I got a peek. You're breathtaking. I love you."

I hear steps moving down the hall and assume Richard's gone.

Staring at the door, transfixed, I can feel Amelia's eyes piercing two holes between my shoulders.

She's right. I know Richard. I know where I stand with him. Jake? I don't know him anymore. It hits me like a punch in the stomach. It's been too long. The Jake I knew wouldn't have married a woman to divorce her only months later. Maybe he's a different man, altered beyond all recognition. He won't be the same Jake I once knew. The boy I lost my virginity to one summer afternoon at his parents' lake cabin. Amelia's right—I'm not going to throw everything away for the memory of something that's long gone.

Thirty-one

Vows

♥♥♥

Saturday, September 1—Chicago Area

On my wedding day, I wake up when it's still dark outside. It takes me a couple of blinks to remember why my heart's beating so fast and why my entire body seems to be sparking with electricity. *I'm marrying Jake today.* I savor the thought, snuggling under the warm blankets in a cocoon of sheer happiness.

My solitary bliss is short-lived. A few minutes later, alarm clocks come to life around the house and everything seems to explode in a bustling mayhem. Neighbors and friends scamper in and out of the house like little ants along with makeup and hair professionals. It's as if the entire block's celebrating. I glide through everything with a smile on my lips until it's time to drive to the lake.

The inside of the lake cabin has been reserved for my entourage. When Mom pulls up the zipper of my gown, I twirl in little jumps, hands tucked in the delicious pockets of my skirt. And Kassandra and Amelia both clap and hug me.

There's a knock on the door and Jake's mom pokes her head in. "You look radiant," she says. "Jake has arrived; we're ready whenever you are."

I smile and nod. "I'm ready. Can you send my dad in?"

"Sure." Susan winks and she's gone.

"You." I point at the others. "Go."

"We'll see you outside." Amelia hugs me again before exiting.

My dad comes in next. "All right, pie. Let's do this."

He offers me his arm and I take it. Outside, it takes a minute for my eyes to adjust to the bright, mid-afternoon sun, and a little longer for my heart to recover from the sight of Jake in a tux, waiting for me under an arch of white roses. We make our way down the beach along the pretend aisle delineated by two rows of white flowers and green leaves. Until we're there. My dad gives my hand to Jake, and the ceremony begins.

I have trouble following what the minister's saying, as I'm lost in the sea of mountain mist and snowstorm of Jake's gray eyes. I notice we've reached the vows part when Jake gently relieves me of the bouquet, passing it to Amelia, to take my hands into his.

"Gemma, I love you. There isn't a time when I can remember not loving you. As someone once said at another wedding, you are my life."

Edward, Jake's brother, cheers at his quote from my wedding-crashing speech and the crowd gives a chuckle or two. Heads turn as those who know what the quote is about, tell the ones who don't.

I fight back the tears as I listen to the rest of Jake's vow.

"Today's the best day of my life because you're here with me. All I want to do is to protect you and make you as happy as I am today for all the days ahead of us. I vow to love you and stand by your side through everything life will throw at us. I promise to laugh with you, and cry with you, to love and honor you. To never let you go again and always find my way back to you, to us. I vow to love you even when it takes you an hour to order a pizza because you read the entire menu then just order a Margherita."

I chuckle and the first tears roll down my cheeks.

"Gemma, you're the person I want to grow old with, the

person I want to see every morning when I wake up and the one I want to kiss goodnight. I promise to give you all of me and to love you, from this day forward, always."

"Jake." I pause to steady my trembling voice. "Today's the happiest day of my life too. It took us a long time to get here, and some crazy moments…"

The crowd chuckles again. This time everyone knows what I'm referring to.

"I love you because you're the best person I know. The kind of person who even a dying animal would trust with the most important thing she had." I wave toward an iPad set on a pedestal. On the screen is our cat sitter in London, who's following the ceremony via Skype with Lucky. She waves Lucky's paw back.

"Today I give myself to you, completely. I vow to love you even when you make me cry with your incredibly romantic words, completely ruining my makeup on our wedding day."

He brushes the tears away from my cheeks with his thumbs.

"Jake, from the night you kissed me for the first time my heart started to ache with how much I love you. It felt like my chest could no longer contain it as if it didn't belong to me anymore. And it didn't; it doesn't because my heart belongs to you. It always has. Even when we were apart, you were always with me. You were my first love and I want you to be my last. You're the only man I've ever loved, and I promise to love and cherish you from this day forward, always."

Ten minutes later, we're husband and wife.

Thirty-two
At the Altar

♦♦♦

Saturday, September 1—London

After I've made my decision to go through with the wedding, it all spirals out of my control. The hair stylist inserts fresh pink roses in my hair, the makeup artist gives my cheeks a last minute brush of color, and before I know it, the wedding march is playing and I'm at my father's side, walking down the long, long aisle. I hold on to him, hoping this walk will be over soon and willing it to last forever at the same time. So I'm not marrying my first love; almost no one does. Nothing wrong with that. I focus my attention on Richard's adoring face. *I don't deserve you.* The treacherous thought slips out of my head.

I'm such a fraud. Richard's face is glowing with love, and not two minutes ago, I was contemplating leaving him at the altar to chase after another man.

We reach the front of the chapel and my dad gives my hand to Richard. I hold tightly onto Richard's strong arm, trying to stop mine from shaking. I try to plaster a confident smile on my face. Richard leads me to our spots in the center of the aisle and the minister opens the ceremony.

"Dearly beloved, we're gathered here on this beautiful day to celebrate the union of Gemma and Richard in matrimony…"

Right, there's no turning back at this point.

As the ceremony progresses, increasingly frequent shivers of panic spider walk down my spine. My palms begin pooling with sweat and I try to inconspicuously dry them on the skirt of my dress. I hope no one notices.

"...In the time that Gemma and Richard have spent together, they've built the sturdy foundation for a lifelong relationship..."

Now, seriously. We've been together barely a year. It hardly qualifies as a sturdy foundation. Lifelong relationship. It gives me pause; I'm committing myself to Richard for life. It's not on a day-by-day basis anymore; it's forever. *Forever!* Tiny beads of sweat make their appearance on my forehead. Why are those huge yellow lights pointing right in our faces? Are they trying to melt us?

"...May you all remember and cherish this ceremony, for on this day, with love, we will forever bind Gemma and Richard together..."

This forever thing again. Why does he keep repeating it? Isn't once enough?

A noise behind us distracts me. It sounds like the chapel's front door opening. Some late guest maybe. I'm tempted to look back, but I'm afraid that if I see an open escape route, I'll take it.

My corset's too tight. I can't breathe. Oh gosh, I'm going to pass out. I can't breathe. I need to get out of this dress; I need out. Out, I need out.

"If there is anyone in attendance who has cause to believe that this couple should not be joined in marriage, you may speak now or forever hold your peace..."

"STOP," I yell at the top of my lungs, surprising even myself. "I can't do this," I whisper. Aw, it feels good to say it aloud. "I'm sorry, I can't."

The minister stares at me in shock and there's a collective intake of breath from the guests. I look at Richard, petrified. I can already see the sad drop of his brows and read the resigned pain in those beautiful eyes. I can't stand that I'm the one who's doing this to him, so I look away. The door, I need to get to the main door. I want to run away and never stop running. I gather my skirts in my hands ready to make a run for it, turn toward the chapel's front door, and my heart positively stops as I spot Jake standing in the middle of the aisle, looking at me as if seeing me for the first time.

Just like that, the rest of the world disappears, and it's just the two of us, staring at each other. I take in all the details of the face I know so well. I see the boy who stole my heart so many years ago standing before me. My first love, my first everything. The only man I ever truly loved. And I do know him, and he does know me. It doesn't matter how much time has passed, I can read it in his eyes. In a moment, everything changes. My heart swells in my chest, suddenly too big, too full of love to be contained. I look Jake in the eyes and a million unspoken words fly between us, the whispers of our past and the promises of a future together.

Jake's lips curl up in an uncertain smile, hopeful maybe, before he says, "You sort of stole my opening line there."

Something half-way between a sob and a chuckle escapes my lips. Out of the corner of my eye, I catch Richard moving a step backward. I dare to look at him again and find his features set, resigned.

"Is this the bloke you told me about the first night we met?" he asks.

"Yes, Richard. I-I'm so, so truly very sorry…"

"It's not your fault. I knew you weren't ready to marry me. I could tell from the moment I asked." His shoulders sag. "I just hoped that if I made it perfect for you, you'd eventually want it as much I do. But you don't. You never have."

"Oh, Richard." I hug him tightly. "One day you'll make one girl really lucky," I whisper in his ear. "I'm just not that girl."

"I know. I've known for a long time. Go, be happy," he whispers back.

I let him go, gather up my skirts again, and sprint down the aisle toward Jake. I take his outstretched hand and together we run out of the chapel into the sunset.

***

Outside, Jake stops behind me and pulls me backward. "If I have to wait another second to do this…" He cups my face and leans his forehead against mine. "I've missed you so much, I love you so much." He presses his lips to mine in a passionate kiss before I can say anything. My knees buckle underneath me and I grip his arms to stay upright. If one could die of happiness, I'd be heading to heaven.

Jake pulls back. "When I found out you were getting married, I got so scared. I told myself I'd leave you alone, that I wouldn't come here today, and before I knew it, I was in the car driving here."

"Jake, I know. I wanted to crash your wedding when I found out, but I couldn't. I-I love you. I love you. I love you." He kisses me again.

"You really wanted to crash my wedding? How? What happened?"

"Later," I tell him, looking over his shoulders at the chapel door as the first stunned guests flood out. "Let's get the car and get the hell out of here, *now*."

He takes my hand again and drags me forward to his car. We're almost there when someone screams my name. I turn around and see Amelia running toward us holding her long skirt in one hand and dragging my honeymoon suitcase behind with the other. She catches up with us in the parking lot and throws her arms around my neck.

"I'm sorry I didn't tell you," she whispers in my ear. "I was wrong."

"It doesn't matter, it's all good now." I beam at her.

"I can see that." She smiles back at me then at Jake. "You stole the bride."

He gives her his best mischievous grin.

"Make her happy," Amelia says.

"Will do." Jake nods. "I'll get the car," he says. "Give you girls a minute."

Amelia seems about to cry. She hands me the suitcase and takes from her shoulder my purse with my phone, wallet, and passport inside. "After being a runaway bride myself, I thought you might need these."

"Thanks. Tell my parents I'll call them soon. And please say sorry to everyone."

"You don't worry about a thing, I'll take care of everything here. Now go and be happy."

Jake backs the car next to us and I climb in the front seat, waving goodbye one last time as we screech out of the yard, sending gravel flying behind us.

"Any idea where we're going?" I ask.

Jake looks at me then back at the road. "There's a flight leaving for Hawaii in two hours. If we hurry, we can catch it."

"Are you sure you didn't plan this?"

He gives me that wicked, lopsided grin I love so much and winks at me.

I take Jake's hand and look at the road ahead, unable to wipe a huge smile off my face. "Woo-hoo. Hawaii, here we come."

Thirty-three

Two Become One

Sunday, September 2—Honolulu

After the beach ceremony, we party all of Saturday night and leave for our honeymoon in Hawaii early on Sunday Morning. We arrive in Honolulu in the evening, the day after the wedding. At the arrivals gate, a guy's waiting for us with a piece of paper saying, Mr. and Mrs. Wilder. The writing sends a thrill down my spine.

Our hotel is in Kapalua Bay and the drive there takes a little less than an hour. Most of the road runs along the coast; we pass several beautiful beaches, and in more than one, wedding ceremonies are taking place in the sunset.

"Do many people come to Hawaii to get married?" I ask the driver.

"Yes, many. One of the easiest places to tie the knot, as easy as in Vegas. You just need to take your license and find a minister."

Cool.

At the hotel, Jake takes care of the check-in while I stare at the ocean from the hotel's lobby. Its waves seem to pull at me, the wind to whisper in my ears as if this moment is somehow a significant one.

We follow a clerk who shows us to our room, the honeymoon suite. While the clerk shows Jake the perks of the room to earn his tip, I feel the pull of the ocean again. I spring the French doors open and walk outside onto the patio. A gentle ocean breeze caresses my skin. I look up at the stars and they seem to wink back at me as if they know something I don't; as if my destiny is written in their constellations. My husband comes up behind me and wraps his arms around my waist.

"Beautiful, aren't they?" he asks, looking up with me.

"You think we were destined to be together?"

"I don't know if it was destiny, fate, sheer luck or whatever. I'm just glad we found each other once and then again."

"It was destiny. I believe that if things had gone any other way, we'd still be here, under these same stars, married, happy."

Feeling as one with the universe, I kiss Jake. He lifts me up, never breaking the kiss, and walks me back into the room, wedding night style. I rest my head on the nook between Jake's shoulders and neck, breathing in his scent. My heart's pulsing with life—a new life I'm going to live with Jake by my side.

♦♦♦

Sunday, September 2—Honolulu

A thirty-hour flight, a visit to the Honolulu Marriage License Office, and a $95 Beach Wedding booking later, Jake and I are standing on a beautiful beach in Maui at sundown, holding hands before a minister. Jake proposed to me in the middle of Heathrow Airport, and on the journey to Hawaii, we talked and talked and talked about everything that has happened to us over the years. We had so many things to say, but it still felt as if we'd only said bye to each other the day before.

"Gemma and Jake," the minister says, bringing me back to present.

I stare into Jake's eyes.

"Congratulations to both of you today," the minister continues. "You should enjoy this special moment in your lives. Today's an exceptional day. Today your memories and hopes merge together. Today they become one. Today the word marriage has a special meaning. It means the end of the search for that special love. Today it brings fulfillment, it brings completion to your lives… Now to the proceedings. Jake, do you today, sir, take Gemma to become your lawfully wedded wife?"

Jake squeezes my hands. "I do."

"And do you today, Gemma, take Jake to become your lawfully wedded husband?"

I squeeze back. "I do."

"Would you please repeat these words after me: to love and to cherish…"

"To love and to cherish..." *we echo.*

"To have and to hold…"

"To have and to hold..."

"To honor and respect…"

"To honor and respect..."

"From this day forward."

"From this day forward."

"Now the rings exchange."

Jake takes out of his jacket pocket two wedding bands we bought at a cheap jewelry shop at the airport.

"You are about to present rings to one another," the minister goes on. "As you can see, rings are round. This circle will remind you that your love shall always be with no end. As you walk together through life, protect your love, always speak from your heart, and listen closely to one another. Cherish every moment you're given together. And you'll strive together with your love for each other. Now, on to the final words. Please repeat after me: with this ring, I marry you…"

"With this ring, I marry you..."

We both put a band on the other's finger.

"I join my life to yours…"

"I join my life to yours..."

"All that I am, all that I have…"

"All that I am, all that I have..."

"All of my love, I gift to you."

"All of my love, I gift to you."

"And now, for the power invested in me by the state of Hawaii, it's my privilege to pronounce you husband and wife. You may kiss the bride."

***

We end up staying in a hotel in Kapalua Bay. The minister suggested this part of the island, and we were lucky enough to find a hotel without an advance booking. Jake takes care of the check-in while I stare at the ocean from the hotel's lobby. Its waves seem to pull at me, the wind to whisper in my ears as if this moment was somehow a significant one.

We follow a clerk who shows us to our room, they gave us the honeymoon suite. While the clerk shows Jake the perks of the room to earn his tip, I feel the pull of the ocean again. I spring the French doors open and walk outside on the patio. A gentle ocean breeze caresses my skin. I look up at the stars and they seem to wink back at me as if they know something I don't; as if my destiny is written in their constellations. My husband comes up behind me and wraps his arms around my waist.

"Beautiful aren't they?" he asks, looking up with me.

"You think we were destined to be together?"

"I don't know if it was destiny, fate, sheer luck or whatever. I'm just glad we found each other once and then again."

"It was destiny. I believe that if things had gone any other way, we'd still be here, under these same stars, married, happy."

Feeling as one with the universe, I kiss Jake. He lifts me up, never breaking the kiss, and walks me back into the room, wedding night style. I rest my head on the nook between Jake's shoulders and neck, breathing in his scent. My heart's pulsing with life—a new life I'm going to live with Jake by my side.

♥♦♥♦♥♦♥

Two weeks later, the last day of our honeymoon, Jake wakes me by nuzzling my neck.

"How's my beautiful bride?"

I want to say, "Wonderful," or "Crazily happy," but the truth is I'm feeling groggy at best.

"I'm sleepy. Do we have to start packing already?"

"What's wrong?" Jake's immediately up and alert. He turns on the lights and checks my temperature, placing the back of his hand on my forehead. "You're pale."

"Nothing's wrong. I'm just a bit queasy. Maybe the Lao-Lao from last night was a bit heavy."

"Are you sure?"

I'm about to say yes when I gag. And before I know it, I'm running for the toilet.

Jake's at my side in a matter of seconds and he holds my hair back as I puke. Not the most romantic ending to our blissful honeymoon, but a good insight into that 'in sickness and health' promise.

When there's nothing left in my stomach, I wash my mouth in the sink and sit on the closed toilet to recover.

Jake hands me a damp towel to place on my forehead. "Better?" he asks.

"I just wish I didn't have to fly thirty hours with food poisoning. But I'm fine."

From under my towel, I can see Jake's gone doctor on me. He grabs my wrist and stares at his watch.

"What are you doing?"

"Taking your pulse."

"Why?"

"It's a good indication of body temperature."

"I don't have a fever."

"You feel lightheaded?"

"Slightly."

"Does your back ache?"

"A little."

"Are your nipples more sensitive than usual?"

"Are you being dirty with me right now?" I attempt to make a joke, but he gives me a serious scold. "They are, a little. I should get my period soon. It's normal."

"When was your last period?"

"I have the date on my phone."

He retrieves it from my bedside table and I check the notes. "August 17."

Jake gives me a dreamy smile.

"What?"

"Are you still regular?"

"Yeah, like a clock. Why?"

"You're two days late." His smile widens.

Both anxiety and excitement grip me. "You think I'm…

you mean…" My dizziness worsens. "Are you sure?" A honeymoon baby, it'd be too good to be true—nausea aside.

"You'll have to take a test. I'll run to the resort's pharmacy and see if they have one."

He literally runs out of the room. When he comes back, he's sweaty and a little out of breath. "Here." He hands me the test and gives me some privacy.

We wait for the result on the bed. I'm nestling in between his legs and lying back against his chest, the little plastic stick in my hands. Almost immediately, a vertical line makes its appearance across the horizontal one.

"It's positive!" The strongest, weirdest feeling of joy wraps around me as I lean back to look at my husband. "We're going home as a trio."

Jake's whole face lights up now. "You know what they say? First comes love, then comes marriage and then…"

I don't let him finish as I pull his face down in a kiss. Our first as parents…

Note from the Author

Dear Reader,

Hello! If this is the first of my books you've read, welcome as well. And if you've read my books before, thank you from the bottom of my heart for coming back. It's so good to see you again. I hope you enjoyed *Love Connection* and I'm excited to announce the second book in the series, *I Have Never*, is ready. The new story will follow Richard's adventures after Gemma leaves him at the altar. He was too gorgeous a character to abandon like that. Another favorite character will make a guest appearance. Keep turning the pages for an excerpt.

Now I've to ask you a huge favor. Whether you loved or hated *Love Connection* please consider leaving a review on the retailer website where you purchased the book or Goodreads OR Instagram or wherever you like to share your bookish thoughts. Reviews are the biggest gift you can give to an author, and word of mouth is the most powerful means of book discovery.

Thank you for your support!

Love,
Camilla

Acknowledgments

First, as always, I'd like to thank you for reading this book and for making my work meaningful.

A special thanks goes to my online family: book bloggers, the book-loving community, and my Street Team in particular. Thank you for all your help and support.

Many thanks to my two editors, Alison Jack and Helen Baggott.

Thank you to my beta-readers Alex, Desi, and Lily.

Cover images credits: Designed by Freepik.

CPSIA information can be obtained
at www.ICGtesting.com
Printed in the USA
LVHW032208050720
659806LV00003B/189